The money, Stan, Big Lauren & Me

Joanna Nadin

Piccadilly Press • London

For Rik Mason,
who once inspired a street,
and now inspires a whole world

First published in Great Britain in 2011

A catalogue record for this book is available from the British Library

ISBN: 978 1 84812 227 7 (paperback)
978 1 84812 228 4 (ebook)

1 3 5 7 9 10 8 6 4 2

Printed and bound by CPI Group (UK) Ltd, Croydon, CR0 4YY
Cover design by Simon Davis
Cover illustrations by Sarah Kelly

My World

by Billy Grimshaw-Jones
Year 6, St Laurence School

My name is Billy Grimshaw-Jones. It used to be just Billy Grimshaw, but my mum got married to Dave last year and so now we're double-barrelled, which Stan who is my little brother says makes us sound rich but we're not really. We could have been if Mum had married say Shane Watts who is the Number 7 for Rovers and who lives in Rigby Mansions, but we live at 23 Brunel Street and Dave is a nurse and Mum is on the ticket desk at Jetways so we're just average. But if we sell our house, which is 99.9 per cent likely according to Enderby Estate Agents but only 70 per cent likely according to Google, then we're moving to 17 Mornington Road which has four bedrooms and an ensuite. We need an extra bedroom because Mum's having a baby. It's due to come out on the 30th of May which is in nine weeks and five days. Mum and Stan want a girl and Dave wants a boy. I'd rather have a puppy. My nan, who is seventy-six and who lives at 20 Beasley Street which is one road away from us, says we should get a cat because they are less bother and don't need walking. This is because her cat who is ginger and called Tammy even though it is a boy doesn't do any exercise. It does a lot of watching horse racing and *Murder She Wrote*. She did have a cat called Dolly but he died and is buried in a Walkers Prawn Cocktail crisps box in our back garden which is why Nan doesn't want us to move. Also Nan says being near family is more important than an ensuite but Mum doesn't agree. Nor does Lauren Hooten who is my best friend and who lives on Beasley

Street too. She says all celebrities have ensuites, e.g. Victoria Beckham and Prince William. She read it in a magazine. She is always reading magazines. And watching *Glee*. We don't watch *Glee* because it clashes with *Man Versus Food* which is on Sky TV and what happens is an American man called Adam Richman has to eat say 180 oysters in not very much time without being sick. It is Stan's favourite programme and my second favourite after *Mythbusters* and Dave's third favourite after *Doctor Who* and *Stargate Atlantis*. Mum says I'll have to stop watching telly when I go to big school in September because I'll have too much homework. But Lauren says last Wednesday she went round to see her cousin Gethin Davies who is in Year 9 and who once got a fork stuck in his hand, and he had done his homework before even *The Story of Tracy Beaker* which is on CBBC. Lauren knows everything about big school, e.g. you can't call it big school you have to call it secondary or you will get your head flushed down the toilet. I would rather stay at St Laurence because even though Kyle Perry once stamped on my Leonardo, who is a Ninja Turtle and who is in charge when Splinter isn't around, he has never flushed my head down the toilet. Or maybe I could not even go to school at all like Clara who is rich and in a wheelchair and is in *Heidi* which is Stan's favourite book at the moment. She has a govarness which is like your own private teacher just for you, and the rest of the time she is just ill. If we were rich, like if Mum had married Shane Watts, maybe I'd have a govarness. I wish I was rich instead of just average.

Monday
23rd March

Everything has gone wrong, just like Nan's friend Brenda Gilhooly said it would. She read it in my tea leaves after school, i.e. she saw a hat at the bottom of the Charles and Diana mug. Nan said it looked more like a tent to her which means a holiday, but Brenda said it was definitely a hat and that meant CHANGE. Nan said that didn't definitely mean a BAD change, it could just be about the baby or moving house, but Brenda said the last time she saw a hat George Clooney left *ER* the next day and it was all downhill from there. Stan wanted his fortune read then, but he had Cup-a-Soup and Brenda said she can't see anything in cream of vegetable.

And when Mum picked us up I knew Brenda was right because Mum's eyes were all red, which was clue number one. Nan said, 'Hormones playing up, Jeanie? That's what happens when you have babies.' But Mum said it wasn't her hormones and anyway she had already had two babies, i.e. me and Stan so she wasn't completely stupid. Nan did a snorty noise but Mum didn't say, 'Why are you doing that noise?' She said, 'Come on, boys, into the car. And for heaven's sake take those off, Stan.' Because he was wearing Brenda's glasses which are pink with a diamond on the side.

But she didn't tell us what was wrong in the car. Or even after tea, which was fishfingers, oven chips and peas, which was clue number two because we never have oven chips except on Fridays. She waited until Dave got back in the Ford Fiesta Zetec, which was at 5.53 p.m. according to my glow-in-the-dark digital watch, which is accurate to a nanosecond. Stan said, 'Dad's home' even though Dave isn't his genetic dad he is his stepdad, and switched the telly over for *Man Versus Food*. Only I was watching *Mythbusters* and Adam Savage and Jamie Hyneman were about to prove whether or not you can shoot round corners so I turned it back and then Stan turned it over again because he said I could watch it on Plus One but he was already on Plus One because he was waiting for Dave. Then I was about to hit Stan with the remote control when Dave and Mum came in and Mum turned the telly off at the wall, which was clue number three. Stan said, 'But Adam Richman is going to eat the world's biggest pancake stack today!' Only Mum said her news was more important than the world's biggest pancake stack. Stan said nothing was more important than the world's biggest pancake stack, but Dave said, 'Enough, kiddo,' so I knew for sure then that Brenda was right and whatever Mum was about to say was a change, and it was bad.

Stan said, 'Is it the baby? Has it got three legs like in that programme on the Discovery Channel? Or is it a boy?' But Mum smiled then and said we didn't have to worry because the baby was fine and definitely didn't have three legs, but wasn't definitely a girl or a boy. The thing was that Jetways, which is where she works at the airport, is closing after the Easter holidays because of the recession, which is when no one has enough money, so she wouldn't have a job any more. Except Mum didn't say 'closing' she said 'going into liquidation' which she explained wasn't like water but just shutting down.

And that's when I could feel it: the electricity in my tummy. It hadn't been there for ages. Not since the time I thought Sean Hawkes was dead only it turned out he had fainted. Because after that nothing really bad had happened.

Not until now.

Dave said, 'It just means a few cutbacks here and there. It's not the end of the world.'

But he's wrong. It is the end of the world. OUR world anyway. Because without Mum's job we won't just be average.

We'll be poor.

I used to count glow stars when the electricity came

in my tummy. Fifty of them on my ceiling. But Big Lauren said no one at secondary school has glow stars they have posters of Katy Perry and Jessie J and I should take them down if I didn't want to get beaten up, so I did. Instead I just lay on the bed on the Spider-Man duvet and said the shipping forecast. Mr A M Feinstein, who is Nan's friend, and is from Berlin only now he lives on Beasley Street, taught me it. It is on the radio. It divides the sea around Britain into areas with funny names and tells boats where the weather is bad, e.g. 'Dogger, Fisher, German Bight – moderate to calm.' German Bight used to be called Heligoland which I think sounds better, like it is an island in a comic for instance where everyone has jet boots and X-ray eyes, but Mr Feinstein says it is just a big bit of grey water really.

Anyway I said all the areas in order three times but the feeling didn't go away, so I tried to think of things that made me happy, like Dr Singh who is our doctor and who has big hands told me to. So I thought about 17 Mornington Road and about the wallpaper in my new bedroom which isn't spacemen like here it's blue striped which is more grown-up and the staircase which is twenty-seven steps and the gold taps in the bathroom which aren't real gold but that isn't the point.

But then I had another bad thought which was if Mum doesn't have a job then we won't be able to move to 17 Mornington Road at all. So I asked her when she came upstairs and sat on my bed. I didn't look at her because I had tears in my eyes and no one at secondary school cries according to Big Lauren. I just stared really hard at where Stan had picked off a spaceman's helmet on the wallpaper and said, 'Are we still moving?' She said, 'It's complicated, Billy, love. There's not so many jobs out there right now – not for pregnant women anyway,' which meant no. I said, 'I wish you weren't pregnant then or I wish the baby DID have three legs or a tail or something because then it would be a phenomenon and we could be on telly and be millionaires.' Mum said, 'You don't mean that, Billy.' I said, 'Yes I do.' Mum said, 'There's more to life than money, Billy.'

But there isn't. Not at our school anyway.

Tuesday
24th March

You can't shoot round corners. Big Lauren told me on the way to school. Dave said he would give me a lift with Stan because Mum was already at work, but I said no thanks because Stan is wearing a white glove and hat like Michael Jackson again. Dave said Stan can wear a white glove and hat if he likes, even though he isn't black or a pop star, it's all about expressing himself. I said if he expressed himself at secondary school he'd get his head flushed down the toilet. Dave said, 'Don't believe everything that Lauren tells you.' I said I didn't. Like when she said she'd seen a vampire I knew THAT wasn't true. But I told Dave that Gethin says Dane Luton in Year 7 got it done to him just because he had the wrong trainers on. Dave said, 'Christ on a bike,' which is supposed to be 10p in the swear box, but I didn't say anything because I was too busy thinking about being poor and having the wrong trainers.

When we got to the school gates I told Big Lauren about Jetways closing. She said it is like in *Charlie and the Chocolate Factory* when Mr Bucket loses his job and they are even too poor to have cabbage soup. I said Dave still had his job even though he is a nurse and we still had Cheerios for breakfast this morning but she said, 'For now.' Big Lauren said she knows for a fact that Kyle Perry who is on free dinners only has crisps for breakfast because she has seen him outside Mr Patel's with his mum and he has a packet of pickled onion flavour Monster Munch and his mum has a Benson and Hedges cigarette. Plus they don't shop in a normal supermarket like, e.g. Sainsbury's, they shop in Discount Deals which is where you don't get beans with Heinz on them they just say *Beans* and they don't taste right. I said I don't really like beans I prefer spaghetti letters. Big Lauren says they don't have those in Discount Deals at all.

Then it got worse because when we got into class Miss Cafferkey gave us our essays back. Mine had a C-minus on it which is better than Kyle Perry who got a D, because his essay said he is related to Wayne Rooney which isn't true. But not as good as Stephen Warren who got an A for writing all about when he gets to watch Rovers training because his uncle is the linesman and when he grows up he wants to be an international football star or maybe a linesman too. Miss Cafferkey said if I had spent more time focusing on the things I do rather than on how much they cost I would have got a better mark. Plus I spelt 'governess' wrong and forgot to use enough commas. I asked if I could do it again, but she said no because they are all being sent to our new teachers at secondary school so they know about us and about our abilities. And then I could feel the electricity again because I knew my essay was a lie because we won't be moving and Mum won't be working at Jetways and we won't be average at all and then they will put me in a class for poor children and I will get my head flushed down the toilet for sure. Miss Cafferkey said, 'Do you need to go and see Miss Butterworth, Billy? You look a bit peaky.' But I said no thanks because Miss Butterworth who is the school secretary and also the nurse would ring Mum. And also because I had had my idea.

It just popped into my head, which Mr Braithwaite, who is our headteacher and is called Wing Nuts because his ears stick out like wing nuts, says is a lightbulb moment. Like suddenly the words were shining all bright and lit up in front of me. And the words spelt, *Make Your Fortune, Billy*. Because then it won't matter when Mum loses her job. Because I'll be able to buy 17 Mornington Road and a puppy AND the right trainers.

So that is what I'm going to do. I'm going to make my fortune.

Wednesday 25th March

Stan wants to call the baby Taylor. He said it at break-fast when we were having our Cheerios, which are still actual Cheerios and not pretend ones and there is still a half a box left so it is all right for now. Mum said she'd add it to the baby's name list but I can tell she isn't keen because she looked at Dave and so I did too and I saw him roll his eyes. This is because Stan has already added five names to the list and they are Jaden, Harper, Tallulah, Cheryl and Heidi and Dave said no child of his is being named after a goatherd. I said it was inside Mum so she should get to decide but Mum said we're all in the family so we all get a say and did I want to add anything. I said no thanks and Mum looked at Dave again but he didn't roll his eyes this time he just shrugged, and I don't know what that means.

When I told Big Lauren after school she said I was mental and I should have said Lady. This is because Lady Gaga is her favourite celebrity of all time at the moment. Last week it was JLS and before that it was Leona Lewis. But I said Lady isn't really a name plus her new hamster is called Lady and it would be weird having a baby and a hamster called the same thing. Lauren said maybe she could call the hamster Ashley again like the last one who is lost under a floorboard in the dining room, but I said that's OK because what if Ashley 1 came back? And anyway Mum isn't keen on Ashley because it's unisex, i.e. it can be a boy or a girl, e.g. like Lesley or Charlie. Lauren said Billy is unisex and I said it wasn't and she said it was because of Billie Piper even though it's spelt wrong. And then I didn't want to talk about names any more so we looked at her magazines which are all about celebrities who are kissing other celebrities or have stopped kissing other celebrities and got fat, and make-up and diets. Lauren is on a diet again. She says she has to lose a stone before secondary school or no one will talk to her. I said I would talk to her but she said if I do then I will probably get my head flushed down the toilet. Everything seems to end up with my head getting flushed down the toilet. Lauren said that's what puberty is all about. I haven't done puberty yet because I am the second youngest in our year, but Kyle Perry has started because he has some hair down there, and so has Kelly Thomas because she wears a bra and she is only ten. Big Lauren wants to wear a bra. So does Stan. He is always trying on Mum's when she's getting dressed. I said he had to stop it because what if someone finds out and beats him up or beats me up? Mum said I was being dramatic again and it's fine for him to experiment, but that wearing a bra isn't all it's cracked up to be and he is lucky to be a boy and not to have to put up with all that shenanigans. This is because the baby has made her be sick every morning and also she has to wee at least three times in the night, but Stan said he wouldn't mind.

Sometimes I wish he wasn't my brother. Even though it was him who found the competition.

It was on page ten underneath a picture of Vanessa Hudgens in a bikini. All you had to do was say where Paris was, was it in a) France b) Germany or c) America and you could win £10,000 or a bottle of pink nail varnish and I know it is in a) France because Big Lauren says Paris is the romantic capital of the world because they speak French not English, and she is getting married there or maybe in the registry office on Park Road. And then I had the idea which was that we could enter the competition and win our fortune. Lauren said she was always entering competitions to win stuff and all she had got so far was a *Rainbow Magic* fairies book, so we would probably only get the nail varnish if we were lucky. But Stan said if we entered all the competitions in all the magazines then we would win something for sure.

So we did. We filled in all the forms and looked up

all the answers on Google which I said was cheating because you are supposed to just have them in your brain, but Big Lauren says this is modern life, and if we win them all we will get:

£10,000

A year's supply of baby wipes

A romantic minibreak for two in the Lake District

A caravan

A subscription to *Women's Own* magazine

A CD of Neil Diamond

A set of steak knives

A Toners hair dye in 'Mahogany Shine'

I said it wasn't worth doing the last three because no one likes Neil Diamond, Dave is a vegetarian and Mum doesn't dye her hair because of the chemicals and the baby but Stan said we could always sell them on eBay because Arthur Malik's mum just sold his old Scalextric on eBay and she got £31.50, and Big Lauren said her stepdad Alan sold a sock that was once on Andy Murray's foot and he got £372.

I got the stamps off Mum. She said why did I need

so many and I said it was for something for the baby. Which was only half a lie because if we win then the baby will have proper baby wipes instead of Discount Deals ones. And she smiled then and said, 'That's nice, Billy.' And I felt a bit funny then. Because she hasn't said that in quite a while and it felt good and scary at the same time. Because what if we don't win anything and the baby doesn't even have any wipes at all?

But then I remembered that one of the magazines said it is important to always think positive. So I did – I thought positive and the thought was, all we have to do now is wait for our fortune to arrive in the post.

Thursday 26th March

Everyone at school has gone *Britain's Got Talent* mad. It's because there's an advert in the *Broadley Echo* and it says there's a big audition in Bristol which is near here and it's in four weeks and if you have hidden talent it's time to show it to the world, and also to Ant and Dec who are the presenters and Simon Cowell who is the judge.

Karen Connolly is going to go and sing 'It's Raining Men' while she dances with an umbrella and Casey Webster who once got stuck in a washing machine is going to swallow a live goldfish. Big

Lauren said that was animal cruelty but Casey said he doesn't kill the goldfish it is a trick because then it comes back out of his mouth again and it's totally amazing and he will win for sure. Miss Cafferkey asked if I was going to enter but I said I don't have any hidden talents. She said, 'Everyone has talent, Billy, you just have to find yours.' So I said I was good at identifying car makes and models from a distance so maybe that was mine, but Simon Cowell would press the no buzzer for sure if I did that.

But on the way home from school, Big Lauren said that her cousin from Swansea – not the one who got knocked on the head and goes to special school but his brother – won a talent show at Pontin's Holiday Camp and he got £500 and a silver trophy, and that if we won *Britain's Got Talent* we would get more than that and so we should be in a band and enter. I said what about the competitions in the magazines, but Big Lauren said it is like boyfriends, i.e. you have to keep your options open.

We did it at my house. Because Mum and Dave were on shift and Nan can't have us on a Thursday because she's at bingo with Brenda Gilhooly so I have a key which is attached to a string which is attached to a clip on my school bag so I can't lose it and I bring Stan home. We're allowed to make ourselves cold drinks – NOT hot chocolate – and a snack and watch telly and not answer the door but we can answer the phone until everyone gets home.

Only we didn't actually do singing because it took too long to decide what to be called, i.e. Lauren wanted to be called Lady Lauren only I said that made it sound like it was all her and what about Double Decker because there are two of us, only Lauren said no because Double Deckers are big buses and she doesn't want to draw attention to her diet, but how about Double Trouble? I said but that makes us sound like we're bad and we're not, but then Lauren said I was being sexist by not letting her decide so we're called Double Trouble and Lauren is going to sing 'Pokerface' and I'm going to join in on the 'P-P-P-Pokerface' bits and do the dance routine.

Stan wants to be in Double Trouble too because he says you always win with someone really small in the band, e.g. Diversity, but I said no because then it won't be Double it will be Treble and Treble Trouble sounds weird, so he said he was going to ask Mum when she got home and she will say yes and then I will have to let him in. But Big Lauren said rehearsal was over anyway because she had to go and put Lady the hamster in a see-through ball and let her roll around the front room for a bit and so I watched *Mythbusters* and it turns out you can make a deadly weapon in prison with pant elastic.

Friday
27th March

Mum said me and Big Lauren should let Stan be in Double Trouble. I said it wasn't fair because no one made Cheryl Cole let her brother in Girls Aloud and Dave said maybe that's why he ended up in prison. And then Stan got upset in case he went to prison so Dave said he would be in a band with Stan but Stan said no because Dave can't sing, not even 'Happy Birthday'. Mum said no one was going to enter *Britain's Got Talent* at this rate, but I said we had to and we had to win. I must have said it quite loud because Dave said, 'Blimey, keep your hair on,

25

Billy the Kid.' I said my hair was on. And Dave said, 'Not like Brenda Gilhooly then,' because she wears a ginger wig and you can see the net bit underneath and sometimes when she is laughing it goes down on one side. Mum said, 'Dave,' in her voice that is normally for me and Stan when we have done a really loud burp at the table for instance, and he rolled his eyes at me and I felt a bit better then.

But it didn't last long because then Nan came round because she had won some money on the bingo and it was £100 and she tried to give it to Mum, but Mum said, 'Christ, we're not on the breadline yet.' So Nan said, 'Suit yourself. I'll put it in the coffee jar then.'

She has £174 in three coffee jars. There was £176 but she used two pounds to pay for the ice cream van last week because she only had a twenty-pound note in her purse and Mr Whippy doesn't like twenty-pound notes unless you are buying say fifteen Cornettos. No one would do that, not even Big Lauren. She says she once ate three Magnums in a row at Newquay, but she was sick in a Snow White bucket and her stepdad Alan had to rinse it out in the sea.

Nan went home after that and I Googled bread-line. It's where poor and homeless people queue up for food.

I don't ever want to be on the breadline. Not even if it's sliced white.

Saturday
28th March

It's all right for Big Lauren. She says she'll never be on the breadline because her mum works at the betting shop on Whitehawk Road and she says the recession is good for betting because more people want to win money, e.g. Kyle Perry's dad Mr Perry who is in there every lunchtime and a lot of Saturday. Last week Mrs Perry who is Kyle Perry's mum was in there too only she wasn't betting she was shouting at Mr Perry. Big Lauren says more couples argue about money than anything else and it's the number one cause of marriage breakdown.

I said Mum and Dave weren't arguing any more than normal, e.g. only stuff like, 'It's your turn to do the bins.' 'No it isn't I did them last week.' 'Yes, well I'm pregnant.' Which wins every time except when it was about making a cup of tea because Dave said being pregnant wasn't a hindrance to turning on the kettle.

Lauren said it's only a matter of time though.

And she was right, i.e. it was only a matter of three and a half hours. Because Saturday night is pizza night and so we went to Slice O' Heaven on Mason Road and normally Dave has Vegetable Feast and me and Stan share a stuffed-crust Pepperoni Dream only the pepperoni is all on my side because Stan says it's too spicy. Mum has lasagna and garlic bread with cheese on it and a salad, but tonight she didn't want any garlic bread even without cheese or salad or even Diet Coke, she only had tap water. Mum said she didn't feel like it, but I think it was a lie because Dave said, 'Have the garlic bread, Jeanie.' Mum said, 'I'm fine, Dave. I'm just not that hungry.' And Dave said,

'Jesus, Jeanie, it's just a piece of garlic bread, it's not going to break the bank.' And then Mum's eyes got wet and she had to go to the loo and when she got back she didn't talk any more not even when Dave offered her a piece of Vegetable Feast with three olives on it.

Dave says the baby is making her cross. It's huge now and you can see its legs and toes under the skin on her stomach. It's like in the film *Alien* only with a baby not a flesh-eating monster. Stan keeps asking how it got in there, but I am not telling him. I don't want to think about it, or about how it's going to get out. Big Lauren says when she has a baby, which is going to be after she has won *Britain's Got Talent* and married Justin Bieber in Paris, she is going to have a caesarian which is where they cut the baby out of you, or possibly adopt a brown baby from Africa.

I am never having a baby if I get married. What's the point? All they do is make everyone shout at each other and run out of money.

Anyway, when we got home Mum said she was tired and went to bed even though it was only eight o'clock but Dave wasn't tired so he read Stan some *Heidi* and then we watched *Money Madness* which is a quiz show where you can win a million pounds if you answer sixteen questions right. It's mine and Dave's favourite quiz show because the host who is called Hutch Hathaway is always saying, 'It's madness,' and me and Dave are allowed a chocolate button every time he says it. Nan doesn't like Hutch Hathaway because he is American and she says Americans are always up to no good and so are people with beards. She used to say Dave was up to no good even though he didn't have a beard and was from Swindon, just because he wanted to marry Mum. She likes him more now though.

Tonight it was a man from Nottingham called Bob Johnson and he got to £250,000 because he knew things like who was the Prime Minister at the start of World War One, which is Herbert Henry Asquith. And how many pence in a guinea which is 105 but then Hutch asked him who won the Wimbledon Ladies Singles in 1988 and he didn't know so he phoned his friend who was called Una and she said it was Martina Navratilova. But Dave said, 'Muppet. It's Steffi Graff.' And Dave was right, which meant he would have won half a million pounds.

Which is when I had my next idea to make my fortune which was to enter Dave on *Money Madness* and win a million pounds.

I did it on the website. I just had to type in his name and address and answer a question in less than one minute and the question was, *Who was the fifth Doctor Who?* and it's Peter Davison and the computer said, *Congratulations, you are one step closer to a cool million. Keep an eye on the post for your golden ticket to glory.*

So now there are three options open for fortune, i.e.:

Winning £10,000, baby wipes, caravan, romantic holiday, etc in the magazines

Winning *Britain's Got Talent*

Winning *Money Madness*.

I would rather win *Money Madness* because then we would be richer even than Shane Watts and Mum would be able to have garlic bread with cheese every day if she fancied.

But maybe it would be good to get the romantic holiday too, for Mum and Dave. Big Lauren says having a baby is the end of romance. She read it in a magazine.

Sunday
29th March

We did more rehearsing today, i.e. we did 'Pokerface' on Singstar and then 'Bad Romance' which Lauren says is all about her life. Only I don't know how because she has never had a romance, unless you count when Stephen Warren kissed her at the end of term disco, which I don't because it was dark and he said he thought she was Kelly Watson.

But then Lauren said she needed to preserve her voice for the actual audition and we should watch a film instead and it should be *Titanic* because it's her favourite ever film and she has seen it thirty-one times, thirty-two including today. It has Kate Winslet in it who is Rose and who is very rich and Leonardo di Caprio who is very poor but he is going back to America to seek his fortune by doing paintings, only the boat crashes into an iceberg before he gets there. If I was going to America to seek my fortune, only not by doing paintings because I am usually a C-plus at art, but by naming all the states in less than five minutes for instance, I would fly because statistically you are more likely to be killed by a donkey than die in a plane crash.

Maybe I will have to go to America because I don't think we are going to win *Britain's Got Talent* because Big Lauren only scored Wannabe on Singstar which means she doesn't sound like Lady Gaga at all. She says it's not all about the sound it's about the style so she is going to wear a leotard and a hat shaped like a lobster.

But I don't think Simon Cowell will vote for a leotard and a hat shaped like a lobster.

Monday
30th March

Kyle Perry has got a black eye. He said he walked into a door, but Big Lauren said that is what all victims of domestic abuse say but actually it means their husbands beat them up. She read it in a magazine. So then Kyle Perry said to her, 'Are you saying I'm gay because if you are I'll give YOU a black eye,' so he got sent to Wing Nuts for using threatening behaviour. Big Lauren said it's probably his dad that gave him the black eye because according to her mum he lost £150 on the horses yesterday. But the good thing is no one will beat Kyle up at secondary school because they will think he is hard. Stephen Warren said she was being sexist and maybe it was his MUM that gave him the black eye and it isn't hard at all to be hit by a woman. So I said now HE was being sexist and maybe Kyle did just walk into a door because he is usually listening to an MP3 player and not concentrating on where he is going. Only then Miss Cafferkey said she didn't know who was being sexist, but we were definitely all being silly. And also if we didn't be quiet we would ALL get sent to Wing Nuts only she didn't say Wing Nuts she said Mr Braithwaite. So we shut up and did fractions instead and I thought I was glad I wasn't Kyle Perry because even if Mum is pregnant and Dave is too short and a nurse and vegetarian, they have never given me a black eye.

Tuesday
31st March

Sky TV has gone.

I know it was there last night because we watched *Man Versus Food* and it was whether Adam Richman could eat a pizza bigger than a table and the answer was no which means Adam Richman says, 'In the battle of man versus food, food won.' Even Dave was surprised at this because Dave 2 who is Dave's best friend and is also a nurse but comes from Bolton and has a tattoo of Daffy Duck on his arm, once ate two sixteen-inch Meatastics in one evening. Only he won't do it again because he is getting fit so he can become Ultimate Frisbee Champion, which is also why he doesn't play WarRaiders any more. I said maybe I could become Ultimate Frisbee Champion and win a million-pound prize but Dave said Dave 2 has only won a silver frisbee so far plus you have to be at least eighteen. And mental.

But when I got back from school with Nan and Stan it had disappeared, because I went to put *Mythbusters* on so I could find out whether a thousand bees can lift up a laptop only it wasn't there and there was just normal telly, i.e. CBBC. I didn't want to watch *Tracy Beaker* although Stan did because he is obsessed with being an orphan and living in a care home because you get to paint your bedroom whatever colour you want and eat sweets all day according to CBBC. Nan said someone must have stolen the satellite dish from off the back wall because that is what happened to Brenda Gilhooly right in the middle of her watching *Haunted House* so you can imagine how terrified she was and it was probably gypsies because Nan thinks gypsies steal most things even though Dave says it's racist to think things like that. Anyway, I went on to the multicoloured gravel out the front to look at the roof and it was still there, so it wasn't gypsies and Nan said it's gremlins then, and Mum could sort it out when she got back from work.

But Mum didn't sort it out. She just said, 'I said we'd have to cut back, Billy, and forty-seven pounds a month is too much to pay just so you and Stan can watch a man eat himself sick and Dave can watch Rovers lose at football.' I said, 'But what about *Mythbusters*? How am I going to know whether or not a thousand bees can lift a laptop?' and she said, 'Google it.' And even though I totally like Google I don't like it as much as Sky TV and I could feel the anger pushing up inside me until I pushed out some words and they were, 'I hate you and I wish I was dead,' and the words were like Kyle's dad's fist, or peas out of Stan's pea shooter because every time one hit her I could see it left a mark. But I didn't care I just went to my room and I said the shipping forecast five times and waited for Mum to come up and say sorry but she didn't and nor did Dave and nor did Nan.

And then I thought maybe they are pretending I actually am dead. And then I wished I was Kyle Perry. Because at least his mum doesn't pretend he is dead.

And he still has Sky.

Wednesday
1st April

A thousand bees can't lift up a laptop because one bee can only lift ninety-six milligrammes so it would need 23,000 bees and anyway how would you attach the harnesses? I Googled it in first break and I was going to do it as show and tell, even though it's just tell really because I don't have a bee not even a dead one. Only Miss Cafferkey said not today Billy because she wanted to talk about our new project for after the holidays. It's The Victorians which is 150 years ago when Queen Victoria was in charge and there weren't any laptops or Sky TV or even any television at all and only the rich children went to school like, e.g. Brooklyn Beckham and the poor ones had to go up chimneys and work in factories. Miss Cafferkey said even Charles Dickens who was a writer and who wrote *Oliver* which is where they sing 'Food Glorious Food' had a job, i.e. he put labels on shoe polish. And Oliver had a job walking behind coffins and his friend the Artful Dodger picked pockets and everyone agreed that would be brilliant, except Miss Cafferkey who said there was plenty of time for jobs when we were older and we were lucky not to live in filthy slums or have to steal for a living. Only Kyle Perry said, 'Speak for yourself,' so he got sent to Wing Nuts, and anyway it's not true he lives in a slum because he has an Xbox, although Big Lauren says she has seen his mum throw a cigarette packet into the front garden which is filthy.

Anyway, at break everyone went pickpocket mad and Stephen Warren got three Go-Gos off Sean Hawkes and Kelly Watson got a Mars bar off Big Lauren, although Big Lauren says it's not hers because she is on a diet. Kyle got a mobile phone off

Stephen Warren only then Stephen went mental because Kyle wouldn't give it back. Wing Nuts had to come and sort it out and Miss Cafferkey said the holidays couldn't come soon enough, and I said they were coming in two days and then it's Easter and Miss Cafferkey said, 'Thank the Lord for that', which I didn't think was very Christian of her to be glad that Jesus had been nailed to the cross so she could be on holiday, but I didn't say it because I didn't want to get sent to Wing Nuts. And also because I was thinking I was quite glad it was the holiday too because then maybe I could get a job like Oliver or Charles Dickens and make my fortune.

Only when I got home I asked Mum and she said children aren't allowed to work until they are thirteen and I checked on Google and it's true, and also they are not allowed to deliver milk or work in a factory until they are sixteen. I said it wasn't fair so Mum said she'd give me a pound to wash the Toyota Corolla, but I said that was pointless because then the money just goes round in our family and it needs to come from someone who isn't in our house. Mum said, 'Suit yourself.' She is in a mood because she has been down the job centre to see if there is a job that isn't at Jetways, but the man said there isn't anything for anyone in her condition even though Mum said she isn't ill, she's pregnant.

Miss Cafferkey was wrong when she says life was worse in Victorian times, because no one cared back then whether you were ten years old or if you were pregnant, you could work seven days a week if you wanted.

Thursday
2nd April

Something really BAD happened today. And not the kind that means good, which is what Kyle Perry is always saying, like 'My watch is totally bad, innit,' but the kind that means actually BAD.

It's because I answered the door when Mum and Dave were out and Mum said never to answer the door unless I can see through the spyhole and it's definitely her friend Stacey or Gran. I could see it wasn't them because Gran has purple hair and Stacey is orange (because she says without a tan she looks like a corpse which is a dead person but Mum doesn't agree).

But I still did it.

We were watching *Tracy Beaker* and eating our snack which was Cheestrings and Ritz crackers and not even arguing about whether Cheestrings are actually cheese and the doorbell rang and it has thirty-five different tunes and this one was 'Rock of Ages'. Stan said is it Nan or Stacey and I looked through the spyhole and all I could see was some blue suit so I said no and we watched Tracy have another argument with Elaine the Pain. Then the door rang again and this time it was 'For He's a Jolly Good Fellow'. Stan said maybe it's Dave 2. But I said Dave 2 wouldn't ring the doorbell he would stand at the window and pretend to be a gorilla or just come round the back. Then I had a thought which was what if it was a woman from the magazine telling us that we had won £10,000 and she had the cheque and a photographer right there or even Hutch Hathaway to say that Dave was a step closer to a million because he was going to be on *Money Madness*. And then it was like I had two voices and in one ear it was Mum saying, 'Don't answer the door, Billy,' and in the other it was Hutch saying, 'It's madness,' and they were both shouting but Hutch shouted loudest because he is American so in the end I did answer the door. Only it wasn't Hutch or anyone with a cheque and a photographer, it was a man called Nigel Peabody from Enderby Estate Agents and another man and a woman called Mr and Mrs Greaves who were looking for a two-bed semi with a box room because she is pregnant and it's her first.

Nigel Peabody said, 'Is your mum in? I did call and leave a message but I thought I'd try on the off-chance because Mr and Mrs Greaves want to measure up for curtains because there's no time to waste haha.' I said no and I should have said, 'And also we're not moving because Jetways has gone into liquidation which does not mean it's all like water it means they are closing after the Easter holidays so bye.' But those were not the words that came out of my mouth. The words that came out were, 'She's just popped out but she said to let you in,' and Stan was saying, 'No she didn't,' but I said, 'Ignore him he is mental'. And Nigel said, 'If you're sure.' And I said,

'Yes and can I offer you a biscuit? It's an actual Oreo not own-brand, I checked.' But Mrs Greaves said no thanks and so did Mr Greaves and Nigel was already talking about pelmets and I didn't even know what they were.

And up until then everything was good because another *Tracy Beaker* episode came on telly so Stan didn't say anything else because he was watching Tracy pretend her real mum is a film star, which she is not, but then I heard the Toyota Corolla park and not on the multicoloured gravel but on the road, because Nigel Peabody's car, which was a red Fiat 500 2010 plate, was on the multicoloured gravel.

And that is when it all went bad.

Mum opened the door and said, 'Billy?' And I said 'Yes, Mum?' because I was being polite in front of Nigel Peabody. But Mum wasn't being polite because she said, 'What the flaming heck is going on?' And I could have told her the truth but my mouth didn't want to be polite or even to work any more. It just opened and shut like a fish and my stomach felt sick like there was actually a fish inside

49

it and my legs and arms wanted to swim away to America. Only I couldn't swim but I could run, so I did. I ran upstairs, past Nigel Peabody who was tapping the wall on the staircase, and Mr Greaves who was looking in the bath where there is a blue stain still from where Stan tried to dye himself blue with food colouring, and past Mrs Greaves who was just looking pregnant, and into my bedroom. I shut the door and got under the duvet and said the shipping forecast in my head.

And I said it ten times, over and over. But I still felt all juddery. And then I knew what I needed, and I knew where they were, packed away in a box ready for us moving. But I got them out and climbed on the wardrobe which is out of bounds and stuck them to the ceiling but the stick had gone and some of them kept falling down and so I got my purple sticky-tape dispenser shaped like a snail and sticky-taped them even though we are not supposed to put sticky tape on walls or ceilings because it pulls off the paint, but I didn't care about the paint I just wanted them back.

And I got them. Fifty glow stars like a giant night sky above the bed. I counted them and I counted them until the electricity started to die down and my legs and arms didn't feel like running, and then I turned on to my side and stared at the wallpaper spaceman and wished he would take me with him to Mars or Neptune, but he didn't. Instead Mum came in and sat down on the bed and said, 'That was really stupid, Billy. How many times have I told you not to open the door.' And I was thinking, 'Seven times,' but I didn't say it because I thought Mum didn't really want to know how many times, it was a rhetorical question, which if you ask me is just pointless because why ask a question if you don't want an answer? And I was right because she carried on talking and said, 'What if he'd been a burglar or a murderer?' And I thought that a burglar or a murderer wouldn't ring they would just come round the back like Dave 2 only not do the gorilla thing. But I still didn't say anything because I thought she was still being rhetorical, but she wasn't. She said, 'Look at me, Billy.' So I did. And she said, 'Now listen to me.' So I did that too. I listened and I heard, 'I'm sorry he came round, I should have rung him to cancel the viewing, but it slipped my mind. And I'm sorry we're not moving. But you'd miss this house, anyway.' I said, 'No I wouldn't. Because I'd get an ensuite and anyway I hate this house.' Mum said, 'Well, life is like that sometimes, Billy. It doesn't always have a prize or a happy ending. Sometimes it just goes on and you have to make the best of it.' And she didn't hug me like she normally does. She went out and shut the door and I went back to staring at the spaceman. But I didn't wish to be taken away this time. I made another wish.

I wished for the baby to go away. Because then we wouldn't be so poor and Mum would be able to get another job because she wouldn't be in her condition. And I knew it was a bad thing to think, but I thought it anyway.

Friday
3rd April

Akeem Adams is leaving school. It's because his dad works at Gaskell's which is a factory that makes pies and when you walk past you can smell meat and onion. Only they stopped making them last week, and the factory is shut but the pie smell is still there. Anyway, they're moving in with Akeem's grandma who lives in Mangotsfield tomorrow which means he won't be back after the holidays because he's going to All Saints instead.

Kyle Perry said, 'Good riddance,' because Akeem always beats him at Grand Theft Auto, so he got sent to Wing Nuts again. I wish it was Kyle Perry moving instead. Big Lauren says he is a sign of Broken Britain. I think she's right because his front garden is mostly full of bits of car and some broken concrete and their dog Killer's poo. And one of the windows has been boarded up for six months where Kyle's dad broke it with a tin of tomatoes. Nan says they are a disgrace and letting down the street, but Mum says sometimes life is hard and there are more important things than dog poo.

Big Lauren said maybe we could move in with Nan then we wouldn't have to change schools because she is only one road away. But I said Nan only has one spare bedroom and Tammy the cat sleeps in it because Nan snores and Tammy doesn't like snoring. And anyway we don't need to move into Nan's because we will be moving to 17 Mornington Road because I am going to make my fortune.

But then I had a bad thought which was what if Dave loses his job as well then maybe we will have to move in with HIS mum who I'm supposed to call

Nanna June. Only I don't call her anything because we never see her because she lives in Grimsby which is 244.2 miles away from here.

So I asked him as soon as I got home from school when we were on our own because Mum had gone with Stan to do the big shop. And I didn't want to go because Stan rides in the trolley even though he is too old and it makes him look like a mentalist. I went straight into the dining room and said, 'Are you going to get sacked too, Dave?' Dave said, 'Hang on a minute, Billy boy, I just need to kill an elf,' because he was playing WarRaiders which is his favourite game on the computer. So he killed the elf with his sword of plenty and then he pressed pause and said, 'Come here, kid.' And he meant on his lap only no one at secondary school sits on laps so I didn't come here, I stood right there where I already was. He said, 'Have it your way. But listen, people are going to carry on getting ill, which means the hospital will carry on needing nurses.' I said what about Akeem's dad at the pie factory, but Dave said pies aren't the same as nurses because people can always eat cheaper pies or maybe vegetarian sausages for instance, but you can't get cheaper nurses. I thought, 'But you can get vegetarian ones though.' But I didn't say it because Dave says it's not OK to define someone by what they eat, i.e. not to call Samina Hussein 'Halal Hussein' because she is Muslim. Or Whopper Mackenzie 'Whopper' just because he eats so many burgers. Only I don't know what Whopper's real name is, so I don't call him anything. And also because right then Mum came back with Stan and said, 'Give us a hand with the bags, boys. There's a speciality sandwich in it for you,' which is our treat on big shop day. It's toasted bread with a banana and Dairy Milk chocolate inside which sounds gross but isn't. And so we went to give her a hand. Only when we got to the car I could see inside the boot.

The bags weren't orange like they usually are. And when I looked inside the bags there weren't cans of Heinz Beans or Bird's Custard or Kellogg's Corn Flakes. And the chocolate wasn't Dairy Milk it was a foreign word and the bread didn't have a name on it at all. And I knew then that Mum hadn't done the big shop in the normal supermarket. She had done it in Discount Deals.

Dave said, 'Get a move on, Billy, those sandwiches won't make themselves.' But I didn't care because suddenly I didn't want to eat anything not even melted chocolate and hot banana. I said, 'I've changed my mind.' And Dave said, 'You OK, Billy?' I said, 'Yeah. I've just remembered I've got homework.' And I went up to my room.

But I didn't do homework. I counted the stars and thought about the speciality sandwich and how it wouldn't taste the same. It would never taste the same again.

It would taste of poor.

Saturday
4th April

Mum found the glow stars. Part of Ursa Minor fell on her head when she was picking my pants up off the floor. I said she shouldn't have been in my room because it's MY room, i.e. private. But she said if I picked up my own pants then she wouldn't have had to go in in the first place, but anyway that wasn't the point. The point was that she thought I had given the stars up and she asked if I thought I needed to see Dr Singh again. I said no and also please stop trespassing, and Mum said, 'I give up', which she says a lot at the moment, only she never does.

Anyway, that is when I made the sign. It's in black felt-tip with a skull and crossbones on it and it says, *KEEP OUT – TRESPASSERS WILL BE PERSECUTED*. Only five minutes later Stan walked right in to borrow a Bionicle because he had left his at Arthur Malik's. So I shouted 'Mum,' only she didn't come because she was having another wee which is nine in the past two hours, I have counted. Dave came instead and he said it was pointless putting a sign at the top of the door because it was too high for Stan to read IF he could read words like 'trespassers' which he couldn't, he can only do small words like 'goblin'. Plus he said I did not mean persecuted I meant prosecuted. And Mum said it was pointless putting a sign ANY-WHERE because me and Stan are going to be sharing a bedroom once the baby comes, and she isn't coming upstairs every five minutes to act as judge and jury. Stan said, 'No way, José,' which he learned off Jake Palmer-Thomas who is second toughest in the infants. I said, 'But why can't Stan share with the baby?' Mum said, 'Are you mad?'

which she isn't supposed to say, because Dr Singh said it can be hurtful. And I said, 'No,' and then no one said anything and it was very quiet until Mum said, 'Sorry. I'll talk to you later.' But she didn't talk to us later, she just went round Stacey's and Dave said he would make us beans on toast for lunch with cheese only it wasn't Heinz beans or Hovis bread or Cathedral City cheddar so I said no thanks and went round Big Lauren's because she has Pot Noodle.

Only after Pot Noodle, which was curry flavour and has 353 calories, Lauren said she had some devastating news and that I should sit down, and did I want a cup of sugary tea? But I said I was already sitting down from eating the Pot Noodle and I still had half a glass of Coca-Cola, so no thanks. And then I thought she was going to say that her new hamster Lady was dead, or maybe even Alan. But she said it's that she is going to Florida a week on Sunday to stay with her uncle Garth and aunt Sharon who have two children called Todd and Chip and a house with five bedrooms and a swimming pool and a parakeet. And she won't be back until ten days after that so she will miss the audition for *Britain's Got Talent* and also some school. So we will have to wait until next year to be famous, and why don't we watch *Titanic* again instead. And I said OK because there was no point rehearsing on my own because Simon Cowell isn't going to pick me if all I do is sing 'P–P–P–Pokerface' and spin around a bit.

Plus you would think you would get bored of *Titanic* but really you don't. Even though you know the ship is going to hit the iceberg and start sinking. And even though you know Jack is going to drown because the piece of wood is too small for him and Rose, so he sacrifices himself (which Big Lauren says is romantic but I think is mental because if they had stayed more still they could both have fitted on). You are still hoping that this time it will be different, and that the ship will only flood a bit and Jack will get to America and find his fortune and be rich enough to marry Rose.

But it never is.

The worst bit's at the very end though which is in

modern times when the man on the boat is looking for Rose's blue heart-shaped diamond necklace which is called the Heart of the Ocean. Only it turns out that Rose, who is 101 now which is ancient but not the oldest person in the world who is Japanese and 114, has secretly had the diamond all along only instead of telling anyone she drops it into the sea. How mental is that? Big Lauren says she wishes her grandma had been rich and drowned on the *Titanic* instead of just having a heart attack in a shoe shop. Because if her nan had had a blue heart-shaped diamond necklace, then Lauren could wear it to the leavers' disco next term and it would be better than Kelly Watson's diamanté choker any day. But I said if I had a blue heart-shaped diamond necklace I would sell it and buy the house at 17 Mornington Road instead, because an ensuite is better than a necklace, and even Big Lauren agreed with that. Then she said maybe MY nan had a blue heart-shaped diamond necklace, and I could sell that. But Nan only has a locket with a picture of Grandpa Stokes in and a pasta bracelet that Stan made, and no one is going to buy that. But then I remembered that Granny Grimshaw, who is my real dad's mum, is actually quite rich, which is why she doesn't like Mum or Nan because they are commoner than her. And also why we don't ever see her except when Dad comes back from London, which is hardly ever. But then I thought maybe I could go and see her and maybe she has a blue heart-shaped diamond necklace, or just a diamond necklace not even heart-shaped, and she will give it to me because I am her long-lost grandson like in *Oliver*. Because after Oliver has been at the undertaker's and Fagin's he goes to live with Mr Brownlow, who is his rich benefactor, and he never wants for anything ever again.

So that is what I am going to do. I am going to see Granny Grimshaw and she will ask me to move in with her and be her long-lost grandson and we can watch *Man Versus Food* together because she will have Sky TV and Heinz beans and Dairy Milk chocolate.

And I will be like Oliver. Because I will never want for anything ever again.

Sunday
5th April

Mum isn't keen on going to see Granny Grimshaw. This is because Granny Grimshaw didn't like Mum when she married Dad and especially not when they got divorced. Plus now Mum has Dave's baby inside her so she doubly doesn't like her. Mum said maybe Dad will take me in the summer holidays when he comes to look after me and Stan when her and Dave go up to Dave's sister's in Wigan (we can't go too because there is only one spare room and Mum says no Stan can't sleep in a cupboard like Harry Potter). But I said that's not soon enough it has to be next week, and Mum said, 'Blimey, Billy, what's got into you? It's not like she's going anywhere. She's made of flaming iron, that woman. More's the pity.' So I said I just miss her. Which isn't true because the last time I saw her, which is maybe two years ago, she told me off for wearing shoes on the carpet and for spilling some squash on the tablecloth. And for making the chess pieces play war, even though chess is all about battles according to Wing Nuts, which I said, but she said not with hand-carved ivory ones it isn't. But maybe it will be like in that book *Swallows and Amazons* and she is grumpy Uncle Jim but all she needs is the love of a child, i.e. me. Then she will be all benevolent which means kind, and she will give me a parrot or a blue heart-shaped diamond necklace.

And I said, 'Please, please, please,' about a million times because Big Lauren says it wears them down eventually and she was right because Mum said, 'You win, Billy.' So she rang Dad only his answerphone said he is in France for three weeks and to phone his mobile if it's an emergency. I said it was, but Mum said it wasn't. And I said, 'Is,' and Mum said, 'I am not getting into an argument about it, Billy, you can't go and that is that.'

But then Dave said if it's that important he can take me on Wednesday because he is off-shift that day and Dave 2 is doing Ultimate Frisbee in Derby so he has nothing else to do. So Mum said if Dave was that bored he could start clearing Stan's room or get the car seat from Halfords for when the baby comes, because Stan broke our one by trying to slide down the stairs on it. But Dave said, 'Come on, Jeanie, we've got weeks before the baby arrives and I'm trying to do the right thing here.' So Mum said, 'Jesus. Whatever.' Which is 10p in the swear box, but no one said anything because she is pregnant and is allowed to say what she wants. This isn't fair if you ask me, which I said once, and she said the day boys have to give birth is the day they can start saying being pregnant isn't fair. I hope that day never happens.

And then Stan said was he coming too and I said no because I thought Granny Grimshaw might not feel very remorseful if one of her long-lost grandsons is wearing a Michael Jackson outfit or lipstick for instance, which he did yesterday. But Mum said yes because Stan's best friend Arthur Malik is in Disneyworld so it's the Three Musketeers, i.e. me Dave and Stan or nothing. So I picked the Three Musketeers because like Nan says, beggars can't be choosers.

And even though I am not sat outside the train station with a dog on a string like the 10p man who says, 'Give us ten pee,' all day, and I am not in the slums with Fagin like the Artful Dodger, I am definitely a beggar.

Monday
6th April

Stan won the hair dye. It came in the post this morning and is called Mahogany Shine and is the colour of West Ham's kit but not the blue bit the purple bit. He has begged Mum to let him use it right now, but she said the baby was sitting on her kidneys and the grill was on the blink and the last thing she needed was purple hair dye all over the bathroom and a son who looked like an alien. Stan said he wouldn't look like an alien he would look like Jessie J, but Mum didn't want that either. I asked Mum if anything had come for me, e.g. the £10,000 or the supply of baby wipes or the romantic holiday for two, but she said no just a letter from the council saying she does not get her council tax discount for being a single mum any more because she is married to Dave, and a gas bill. So if I was about to do any complaining then I had better think again. So I did think again and I thought I would go round Nan's.

When I got to Nan's, Mr Feinstein was there drinking tea. I told them both about the big shop at Discount Deals. She said, 'Lawks a mussy,' because she does not trust Discount Deals because it's foreign. But Mr Feinstein, who is foreign and Nan didn't trust him either at first and nor did I, but now we do, said he got his shopping from there and it all tastes exactly the same. And I said no it doesn't. And he said he would prove it and he went home which is opposite Nan's and got a packet of custard creams which didn't even say custard creams on they said, *Fondant Sandwich Biscuits* and Nan got out her packet which said *Peek Freans* on even though she said it was a waste of time because everyone knows Peek Freans are better. And

Mr Feinstein put three of his biscuits on a plate and three of Nan's on another plate and said we had to test to see which tasted better. And I said but I could see that Nan's taste better because they had the right pattern on them and Mr Feinstein's were plain. So Mr Feinstein said it had to be a blind test, i.e. with a blindfold over our eyes which was one of Nan's scarves. Nan said he had better not try to steal her worldly possessions while she was compromised and Mr Feinstein laughed even though Nan was serious.

And Mr Feinstein was still laughing at the end of the test because I picked the Discount Deals biscuits and so did Nan and only Tammy chose Peak Freans even though he shouldn't be eating biscuits at all.

Mr Feinstein said flavour was all in our minds and it's the same with football boots and that just because they are gold or have fancy words on them doesn't mean I will play better or that they are better. But I thought try telling that to David Beckham.

Or anyone at secondary school.

Tuesday
7th April

Mum was off work today. Dave said, 'Is this about Stacey?' Because Stacey rang last night because she has got a new job at FlyBy which is another airline which isn't shutting down, not yet anyway, and it has better uniforms and a badge that says, *Fly Me, I'm Stacey.* And Mum said, 'I'm really pleased for you, love.' But I could see she wasn't because if it wasn't for the baby inside her she could be wearing a *Fly Me* badge too. But Mum said she was just tired and the baby was giving her gyp. And Dave said if it's that bad maybe she should stop work altogether, especially as she only has another few days left anyway. But she said it was just gyp not pre-bloody-eclampsia and besides they needed the money. And no one put any coins in the swearbox then either, not even Dave. He just got his bag and slammed the door and then I heard the Ford Fiesta Zetec start up and Mum went back to bed and me and Stan watched four episodes of *Tracy Beaker* on CBBC because it's Tracy Beaker Day which means that is all there is until five o'clock.

Stan said if Mum and Dave can't cope with us because the baby is too much work then we could move to the Dumping Ground, i.e. the house where Tracy lives, which is actually called Elm Tree House. He said it would be excellent because we could go to an assault course and camping and also trick the care workers into walking under buckets full of water. I said I'd rather move to 17 Mornington Road, but Stan said it doesn't have a common room or bunk beds so he'd rather be an orphan.

And after that I didn't want to watch any more *Tracy Beaker* so I went upstairs to ask if I could go round to Lauren's but Mum was asleep and I thought if I woke her she would shout so I should just go. I did, only Lauren wasn't in she was at the shops with Karen Connolly getting holiday clothes so instead I just carried on walking. I walked and walked, down Park Road past the post office and the registry office and Costcutter where Gran's old cat Barry had died. I walked through the park where Preston Yates who is at secondary school was kicking a football at a bin. I walked across Bellamy Avenue where Sean Hawkes lives and left at the corner until I was there. Until I was standing right outside it.

17 Mornington Road.

I thought maybe I could knock on the door and the owners would let me in and say come and live here anyway, Billy, you can have the big bedroom at the back with the strip wallpaper and the ensuite and the view of Gaskell's which some people say is an eyesore, but which is actually very interesting.

Only they didn't. Because I didn't even get the chance to knock on the door. I didn't even walk up the block paving on the drive. Because when I got there something was wrong. Because on the gate there used to be a big sign that said,

Enderby Estate Agents.

Turning a House into a Home.

FOR SALE.

But this time someone had nailed another piece of wood across it. And this bit of wood didn't say *FOR SALE*. It said *SOLD*. And my heart jumped inside my chest because I thought that Mum and Dave had bought it anyway. That they had won the lottery and not told us so it would be a surprise and that I would get home and Dave would say, 'Guess what, Billy boy, we're moving house tomorrow.'

But that good feeling lasted only four seconds because then I felt someone push past me and say, ''Scuse us, sonny,' and I looked and my heart fell back down again, not just to where it started but even further, deep inside me, where it was dark and cold and black.

Because the voice came out of a man with a blue boiler suit and a bald head and he was carrying a chair only it wasn't the green one with the ripped bit in the cushion that we have to turn upside down so you can see the zip, i.e. Dad's old chair that Dave sits in now. It was brown and leather with a bit underneath that you can whizz up and make it into almost a bed and it was being moved into the house with another exactly matching chair and a matching sofa. And when I looked again there was a mum and a dad and two matching girls who were in matching purple dresses and matching bunches with matching Disney Princess Barbies. One of them said, 'Are you our neighbour?' And I wanted to say, 'No.' And 'Because you're in my house. That's MY house.' But when I opened my mouth just a funny noise came out like a gargle and the mum looked at me like I was Kyle Perry or the Artful Dodger so I shut it again before any more weirdness came out and I shook my head instead and walked back the way I came, with my heart cold and dark inside me and my legs full of anger.

And all the way I said the words over and over, I said, 'Cromarty, Forth, Tyne, Dogger, Fisher, German Bight, Humber, Thames . . .' but the feeling didn't go and I knew I needed to count the stars the minute I got in. Only something stopped me and that something was Stan.

He was standing in the kitchen in just his Incredibles pants and a towel around his neck like a cape only the cape was covered in purple and so was his head and so was his neck and so was the floor. He had done the hair dye after all and now everything was Mahogany Shine.

But he didn't look happy. And he didn't look like an alien or Jessie J either. He looked like Stan with a purple face except where the tears had run down which was face-coloured again. Because he was crying and so was Mum and what she was crying was, 'How the hell am I going to cope with three of you when I can't even get you two to behave for five minutes? One of you goes missing, and one of you dyes himself purple.' And I said, 'I wasn't missing Mum. I was just out.' But I said it quiet and I don't think she heard because she just kept shouting, 'It's a bloody good job we're not moving because who's going to buy a house with a purple kitchen floor?'

And I thought maybe Big Lauren would because purple is her second favourite colour after leopard print but I didn't say it. I didn't say anything. I just went up to my room and shut the door so I couldn't hear and pulled the curtains and pulled the duvet over my head until all I could see was blackness and all I could feel was blackness.

Because I know now what is going to happen.

The baby is going to come and me or Stan are going to go. Because Mum can't cope with three of us. And it won't be like *Tracy Beaker*. There won't be coloured walls or common rooms or cans of Coke whenever we want. It will be like *Oliver Twist*. With rats and gruel and shouting. And I will have to run away and find my fortune with Fagin.

Or wait for my benefactor to find me.

Unless I find her first.

Wednesday 8th April

Dave took us to see Granny Grimshaw today. I wore my oldest trousers. The too-short ones with the rip in the knee, which Mum says aren't even worth keeping for Stan and she is going to take them to the recycling bank when she remembers. But she hasn't remembered, not yet, so it was those and a white school shirt and Grandpa Stokes's flat cap from when we had to dress up as someone famous for World Book Day and I went as one of the Railway Children and Stan went as Maccapacca. Dave said what the blimmin' heck did I think I looked like, the

Artful Dodger? And I said, 'No, duh.' Because I was Oliver not the Dodger. But I felt warm spread inside me like a smile or a flower opening because as long as I looked poor and an orphan then the plan would work and I would be rich by teatime.

Even Stan didn't look too bad because most of the dye had washed out of his hair and face and he was in his brown corduroys which have a massive hole in the bottom from where Mum sewed a tail on so he could be a donkey in the Year 2 Nativity only Arthur Malik stood on it in 'O Little Town of Bethlehem' and it ripped right out.

Big Lauren asked if she could come with us because otherwise she has to go swimming with her mum and her sister Jordan, and last time she went big girls called her 'Fatso', but I said no even though I felt bad because Lauren had sequinned Lelli Kelli shoes and lipgloss on, and Granny Grimshaw thinks make-up is common.

Dave said he wasn't going to stay because it would make Granny Grimshaw feel uncomfortable, and he would just pick us up at four. I was glad because he was wearing a Rovers top and Granny Grimshaw doesn't like football not even City because she says that is common too. Even though this isn't true because how can footballers be common if they are rich? But I wasn't going to say that, not today, I was just going to say I liked tennis instead.

I had it all planned. I was going to admire her four-bedroomed detached house with the through lounge and the conservatory and say how lonely she must be living there all alone and how it wasn't lonely at our house. It was the opposite of lonely, but not in a good way because of the too-many people crammed into the not-enough rooms and maybe she would like someone to help her polish the zigzag wooden floor which is called parquet. I could read *Reader's Digest* to her, which is a magazine for old people, and I could live in the turret like Rapunzel but not with long hair.

Only when we got there, there wasn't any turret and I thought maybe it had been knocked down. Or maybe I was remembering another house from a film, because there wasn't a fountain in the garden or roses trailing round the door. There was something dead in a hanging basket and an upside down recycling bin.

And then it got worse. Because the Granny Grimshaw who answered the door didn't have white fluffy hair and a pink cardigan and pearls like in my head, she had long grey hair that was greasy and a dress with a stain like egg on the front. And she didn't say, 'Why, you look just like William, my long-lost grandson,' she said, 'Who are you? Is it bob-a-job?' which is when Scouts go round and do jobs for money, which used to be called a bob which is 5p, but which is called at least a pound now. And Dave put his hand on my shoulder and said, 'Mrs Grimshaw. I called two days ago. It's Billy and Stan, remember? I'm Dave, Jeanie's husband.' And the 'Jeanie' word must have poked at her brain like a stick, because then she did remember after all because she said, 'Oh, yes. Come in.' And so me and Stan did go in, but so did Dave. And when I said, 'We'll see you at four, thank you Dave,' he didn't say, 'Oh, sorry. See you later, Billy boy.' He said, 'I think I'd better come in after all. Just to be on the safe side.'

And I thought, 'What safe side?' because she is my benefactor who is going to adopt me and let me sleep in a room on my own where none of the wallpaper has been picked off and she will teach me piano and even make me jam tarts.

But now I think that Dave was right. Because the piano was gone. And there weren't any jam tarts. There was a packet of plain biscuits that were soft and tasted of staleness like the wafer I found behind the radiator one time. And Granny Grimshaw wasn't a bit like Mr Brownlow. She wasn't even like Granny Grimshaw, not even the cross one who said, 'How many times, William, no shoes in the house.' She didn't even notice our shoes, not even Dave's, which had a hole in one toe and biro on. She just sat on the flowery chair and drank a cup of tea that Dave made and asked Stan four times if he liked school so that Stan said, 'Like, duh. I already said that.' And Dave elbowed him and Stan said he wished he was at Disneyworld with Arthur Malik or even at the dentist.

And the house wasn't clean and smelling of Glade plug-ins and there wasn't Sky TV on. It was dusty and dark and smelt of bleach and old person and the only noise was a big clock that tocked and tocked counting all the seconds until it was time to go. And every tock was another bit of warmth evaporating and another petal on the flower closing until at four o'clock there was nothing but a dried-up stem and coldness.

Dave says she needs to be in a care home. Like Grandpa Grimshaw who had to go away because he kept walking down to the river with just his pants on even in the snow and he didn't know who anyone was any more not even himself. He told Mum to call my dad to get him to do something about it. Mum said they'll have to sell the house to pay for it probably and Dad won't be happy because that'll be his inheritance gone. And Stan said what about HIS inheritance and Mum said he'd probably get a china dog and Stan was happy because he said Cheryl Cole collects china dogs and maybe he can sell it to her.

And I could hear them saying all this stuff. I could see the words float past me in a long string. But in my head the only words that I was listening to were 'care home'. And the only words I was thinking were, 'That's where you're going too. As soon as the baby comes.'

Thursday
9th April

Nan says she'd rather die than go into a home. She says as soon as they've wheeled you through the door they steal your money and your marbles which means your brains and all you get to eat is mince and it's no wonder everyone gives up bothering to live, e.g. Deirdre Morris who is Brenda Gilhooly's sister went into one called Carnation Drive because she couldn't get upstairs any more and she kept wetting the bed and she was dead within eight weeks and not even Brenda had predicted that. Mr Feinstein said he goes to see his friend Mr Brown in a home called Dorothy

House and he has his own television and a menu for dinner with two choices of gravy, and a lady called Shaniqua does his feet for him once a fortnight. But Nan said she bets Shaniqua is up to no good and that there's arsenic in the gravy. Arsenic is a deadly poison. And Mr Feinstein went home after that because he said sometimes there is no talking to Nan, and also because Nan wanted to go to the betting shop on Whitehawk Road and Mr Feinstein says gambling which means betting is a fool's game and he is no fool. Nan says she's no fool either which is why she only bets five pounds a week, which is less than he spends on seed for the sparrows who can eat stale bread in every other garden, so who is the fool now? But I know neither of them think each other are fools really, because when they watch *Doctors*, which is their favourite daytime soap opera, they are sitting almost touching legs on the sofa and no one else is allowed to sit that close to Nan except Tammy. And maybe me and Stan.

Me and Stan weren't allowed in the betting shop because it's against the law until we are eighteen even though Big Lauren goes in. But it's only to get say seventy pence off her mum for a Mars bar. Nan said we could pick a horse each off the list and she would put a pound on to win and I chose Majestic Rose because of *Titanic* and Stan chose Lady Jameela because it's two pop stars in one and then we sat on the step by the door with a can of Fanta between us and watched everyone go in. Kyle Perry's dad was first and then about ten minutes later Kyle Perry's mum. And then we heard shouting and Mrs Perry came back out again and her face was screwed up like a used-up piece of paper and she was saying swear words to herself. Stan thought it was brilliant but I thought it was at least seventy pence in a swear box. Mr Perry didn't come out. He stayed inside and the next person out was Nan, and me and Stan hadn't won anything and nor had Nan. But Mr Perry had won £450 on a horse called Arnold Lane, which is a stupid name for a horse if you ask me, but no one did. Instead Stan said, 'Why was Mrs Perry swearing then?' Nan says it just goes to show that money does not buy you happiness, e.g. look at Gloria Venables who used to work on the perfume counter in Boots until she won half a million on the Lottery and spent it all on fancy clothes and fancy men. Mr Venables didn't like that so she ended up divorced and cutting pastry at Gaskell's pie factory until that shut, so now she has nothing. Then Nan asked did we want to go to bingo on Mason Road because we are allowed in there. And I was thinking it isn't even true because money CAN buy happiness, e.g. a house with an ensuite or even just custard creams even Discount Deals ones. But I didn't say that, I said, 'Yes, please.'

And the bingo was brilliant because you get a card with numbers on and a fat pen that smells of chemicals and when the man at the front who is called Bingo Jim calls a number out you check your card. If you have that number you put a dot on it with the fat pen and whoever dots everything wins. Only the numbers aren't normal numbers like twenty-three for instance, they are 'Legs Eleven' which is eleven and 'Gordon's Den' which is ten and 'Kelly's Eye' which is one and which doesn't even rhyme. And Nan let us dot her card and she got every single one even before Brenda Gilhooly and so she got to stand up and shout 'Bingo' and so did me and Stan. She won forty pounds which Stan said was a fortune, but I knew it wasn't, not really. But it was still excellent though. Because she didn't put it in a coffee jar, she took us to Slice O'Heaven and we had stuffed crust and garlic bread with cheese and knickerbocker glories for pudding with sparklers in. No one said, 'We can't afford it,' or 'I've paid for it so you have to eat it all'. And I was so busy being happy it wasn't until I was lying in bed again that I felt sick when I remembered about the care home.

And it's one day nearer now because the baby is coming one day sooner.

And I didn't find my fortune. All I got was a nine-inch Pepperoni Dream and an ice cream that I couldn't even finish.

Friday
10th April

It's Good Friday today which is when Jesus was nailed on the cross at Calvary, but I don't see what is good about that at all, it should be called Bad Friday really if you think about it. Big Lauren says but if Jesus wasn't nailed on the cross today then he wouldn't have got up again on Sunday and we wouldn't get Easter eggs, so it's good after all. Then she asked did I want to go into town with her to buy some because you can't get Creme Eggs in Florida, she has checked – plus, Easter doesn't count in the diet because it's a religious holiday. And I said no because I can't afford one, not even a Creme Egg which are only fifty-nine pence, even though I really wanted to because Easter eggs are my favourite chocolate. Mum says they are a rip-off because for, e.g. £3.99 you could buy eight bags of chocolate buttons but instead you just get one small bag inside some normal Dairy Milk chocolate and it's just because it's egg-shaped. But on normal Dairy Milk you don't get a box or foil that smells of chocolate for a month afterwards. Plus egg Dairy Milk tastes better than a bar of Dairy Milk. I have done a blind test like Mr Feinstein so I know it's a fact.

But after about an hour I wished I had gone with her. Because something BAD happened. Not as bad as Jesus on the cross. But almost.

We weren't even doing anything mad. We were just on the computer and I was saying, 'Yes you can build a bridge across a hundred-and-four-foot gap using only duct tape,' and Stan was saying, 'No you can't,' and Mum was saying, 'Oh for crying out loud, I don't know why either of you even want to know about bridges made of duct tape in the first place.'

Only then she said something else, which was 'Oh' in a confused voice. And then she said 'Oh' again but in a different voice, which wasn't confused it was scared. Because there was some red on the front of her skirt and it wasn't hair dye or ketchup or even Stan's Crayola marker pen which is leaking. It was blood. And it was from the baby.

And then stuff happened very fast and slow all at once. Mum had to call an ambulance on the normal phone, and I had to call Dave on her mobile phone and tell him Mum was coming to the hospital and to meet her at A and E, which means Accident and Emergency. Stan had to get her handbag, but he got her the red one which she only uses for parties not the brown one for everyday. I shouted at him and Mum said, 'Please don't shout,' only not in her normal way, i.e. shouting but in a very quiet way and that was when I knew something was really wrong. And it was the baby. The baby was broken. And it was my fault because I had wished for it that time.

I had wished it to go away and now it was going.

★ ★ ★

Me and Stan weren't allowed in the room, we had to wait outside with Dave 2 and it felt like we waited for a million years but it was only an hour and thirty-seven minutes. I timed it on my glow-in-the-dark watch and then the doctor who was called Dr Gupta and who was as short as Dave came out and so did Dave. I waited for him to say the words like they do on *Doctors*, i.e. 'I am so sorry but it's bad news. We did all we could. But the baby could not be saved.'

But he didn't.

He said, 'False alarm. But your mum needs rest and NO stress. Do you know what stress is?' And I nodded because I knew exactly what stress was, and it was me and Stan. And he nodded back, and Dave said, 'You can go in now.' Stan went in and climbed on the bed and showed Mum the syringe he got off Dave 2, but I didn't, I stayed outside because my brain was too loud and crowded with all the thoughts that were in there. The thoughts were, 'This is your fault' and 'You are the stress' and 'Now you are definitely going away'. And they kept going round and round and getting louder and louder until in the end Mum came out and sat on the chair next to me and said, 'I'm OK you know, Billy. I can come home. But I can't go back to work. Doctor's orders. There was only a week left to go anyway.' And the thoughts got a bit quieter then. But they didn't leave completely. They were still there, whispering at me in the car on the way home. And they were still there when Dave made vegetarian shepherd's pie for tea. And when we watched *Finding Nemo*. And when Stan didn't want to go to bed, but he had to because it was gone half-past eight and he knows that Nemo gets back in the end because he has seen it fourteen times, which isn't as many as Lauren's seen *Titanic* but is still a lot.

And they were still there when Mum said what she really fancied was a Bounty only we didn't have any because Nan ate the last one when she came round last week. But then another louder thought came into my head and said, 'You have to look after her. You have to be excellent and kind, and then maybe, just maybe, you won't be the one to go, it will be Stan.' And the thought was right, so I said, 'I'll go and get one from Mr Patel's.' And Mum said, 'Oh don't worry, Billy, it's already dark out. Besides, it's just the baby fancying coconut,' which is odd when you think about it because when babies come out they do not go round fancying coconut. They only fancy milk and crying. But Dave said, 'Let him go, Jeanie. He's eleven, and it's only round the corner. Here's a couple of quid. Why don't you get one for each of us? I think we could all use the sugar after today.' Which isn't true because your brain only needs a teaspoon of sugar an hour to work properly but I took it anyway and I went.

Mr Patel said, 'Bit late to be out, Billy Grimshaw-Jones.' So I said, 'It's the baby. It fancies coconut.' And Mr Patel smiled and said Rupi wanted bananas on toast when she was inside Mrs Patel, only now she won't eat even a mouthful of banana. And babies are funny old things aren't they, and did we have any names yet? I said no because Mum and Dave are still arguing about whether Charlie is a girl's name or a boy's name and whether Willow is brilliant or just mad. And Mr Patel said, 'Sunita is a fine name,' because Mrs Patel's name is actually Sunita, only everyone calls her Sunny, which she is, because she is always smiling. Only there is no way Mum is going to call a baby Sunita, even if it's a girl because Nan would go mental, so I just said, 'I'll tell her, bye.' And I took the Bounties and the change and walked back down Beasley Street towards our road.

But when I got near the corner, which is Kyle Perry's house, I stopped. Because something wasn't normal. Because in the front garden, as well as the bit of old car and the concrete, there were a pair of Chinos and a white polo shirt. The shirt looked orange because of the street lamp at the end of their gate, but no one wears actual orange polo shirts not even Stan. But then another polo shirt came falling out of the sky like a shot bird, and landed on the bonnet of the car, and I looked up to see where the clothes were coming from in case there was a tornado. In tornadoes the wind sucks stuff up and then drops it, and once in France a whole load of frogs fell out of the sky, I saw it on

Weatherwatch. But it wasn't a tornado, it was just Mrs Perry hanging out of the window throwing boxer shorts and a Chelsea top and some books out and she was shouting, 'Go on then, go. I've had it.' And Mr Perry came out of the front door and said, 'For God's sake, woman. Have you gone totally doolally this time?' I thought, 'Probably yes,' because then out of the window came some books and they went further and hit Mr Wrigley's red Vauxhall Astra and two went into Mrs Peason's garden. Mr Perry was shouting at Mrs Perry to stop, but she didn't stop, she just kept throwing things – a radio and a flip-flop and then an envelope which flew right across the road and landed on my trainers. And so I picked it up and was thinking I will just throw it back into the garden or something then they won't even see me when someone did see me and that was Kyle Perry.

He was in the garden and his face was bright orange under the lights and he looked like Mum's friend Stacey or an Oompa Loompa from *Charlie and the Chocolate Factory*. Only in the film the Oompa

Loompas weren't crying and Kyle Perry was because he had orange juice on his cheeks only I knew it wasn't really juice, it was tears. And I wanted to say 'Sorry', even though it wasn't my fault, but just because I felt bad for him.

But I didn't feel bad for long because then he started shouting too and said, 'What are you smiling at Nut-job? Piss off. Just piss off, all right.'

So I did piss off. I ran down the road and over the multicoloured gravel and in the back door and it wasn't until I was hanging up my coat on the hook in the hall that I noticed I still had the envelope in my hand. But I couldn't go back. Not then. Because Kyle had told me to piss off, and because the baby needed the coconut so I thought I will take it back tomorrow. I will just post it through the door really early because Kyle does not get up until ten in the holidays. He just lies in bed and eats crisps and plays his DS, he told Stephen Warren. So I took the envelope up to my room and hid it under the duvet so Mum wouldn't see it and do any worrying.

But I worried. Because, even though my eyes

were watching *Wife Swap USA*, which is where men swap their wives over to see if the other wives are better, and they never are, my brain was thinking, 'There is an envelope in my bed and it's Mr Perry's and what is in it?' I tried to make it go away so I could eat my Bounty bar, but it didn't want to, so in the end I said the baby could have mine as well and actually I was a bit tired and I was going to bed. Mum said, 'Oooh lucky me,' and I said, 'Night' and kissed her, and she said, 'Sleep tight.'

But I didn't. I lay in the dark and I counted the glow stars three times. But all the time I was counting I could feel the envelope at my feet, so I started saying the shipping forecast. I said, 'Cromarty, Forth, Tyne, Dogger, Fisher.' But the envelope started saying things too, it said, 'Look inside me, Billy. You know you want to. What could be inside me?' And I thought. 'It's nothing in there. Just paper and bills.' So I said my words louder: 'BISCAY, TRAFALGAR, FITZROY, SOLE, LUNDY FASTNET.' But the envelope was louder still, saying, 'OPEN ME, BILLY.

OPEN ME, BILLY, OPEN ME, BILLY . . .' Again and again.

Until I did. I opened it.

And that was when I knew nothing would ever be the same again. Nothing. Because it wasn't paper. And it wasn't bills.

It was money. A lot of money.

And no one knew I had it except me and the envelope.

And now the Bad Friday had turned Good.

Saturday 11ᵗʰ April

I couldn't sleep. Because even when I shut my eyes I could see it. The money glowing inside the envelope. Each note shining madly and talking, saying, 'We're yours, Billy, we're yours. All of us. But how many of us are there, Billy?' And I had to know. I had to know how many notes were mine. So I got up and I counted it. I counted it seven times altogether because my hands were all shaky and I kept dropping some and forgetting where I had got to, and getting different numbers. But the last two times I got the same number. I got 5,540.

It's amazing how so much money can fit into such a small space. I thought even a thousand pounds would take up a whole table but it's smaller than a shoebox lid.

And I knew I had to give it back. I knew it wasn't really finders keepers like it is with ten pence. And I meant to, I really did. But things kept happening to stop me, e.g. after breakfast Mum said we all had to go to Dr Singh's because he wanted to check on the baby's heartbeat so I thought, I will take it back after that. But we didn't come straight home we went to the airport so that Mum could get her stuff and say goodbye to everyone because she is never going back now. And then Mum was sad so we went over to Stacey's because she doesn't start her new job for a few days. And Stacey made me and Stan toasted cheese and pickle sandwiches and let us watch Sky while she and Mum did talking in the kitchen. Mum ate her toasted sandwich which was just cheese because the baby doesn't like pickle, and Stacey smoked a Benson and Hedges out of the window because the baby doesn't like that either and nor does

Mum. And then when we got back home which was nearly three o'clock, Big Lauren was there with a cage and Lady and two Creme Eggs, one each for me and Stan, saying, 'Can you look after her while I go to Florida? She only needs feeding once a day and she can be in the front room and she is almost as fun as Sky because she can do tricks, for example she will eat almost anything even her own poo and hang off the bars with one foot and then fall on her head. And here is my uncle and aunt's address so she can send me a postcard.' And Mum said yes and so did I even though I do not know how Lady is supposed to write a postcard. Although she can do excellent tricks. So we were busy watching her fall on her head, and seeing if she would eat her poo until it was time for Lauren to go and tidy her room. She said her mum doesn't want to come back from Florida to a bombsite, plus she can't find her red bikini top, but it's definitely on the floor somewhere.

And then Mum said, 'What a good idea,' because it's nearly time for the move, i.e. for Stan to come into my room. She said Dave doesn't want to be wading through pants and socks and broken Transformers, he wants to just carry the chest of drawers and the bed down the landing and put them next to mine, so we could go and tidy our rooms too. So I did tidy. I put away all my *Doctor Who* Top Trumps cards and my *Cars of the World* books and my collection of fifty-seven different crisp bags. But all the time I was tidying, the envelope was saying things to me from under the mattress. It said, 'You could take me back. Or you could spend me. Think of what you could buy, Billy.' And I tried not to think but thoughts happened anyway, e.g. a DS and new football boots with Reebok or Nike on them and maybe even a new house not 17 Mornington Road because the matching girls are there now but in Rigby Mansions where Shane Watts lives. But then another bit of my brain had a thought too which was, 'But it's not yours, Billy. It belongs to Mr Perry so you have to take it back to him.'

And it was like one of the quizzes in Big Lauren's magazine where it says, *You have found your biggest enemy's purse on the floor outside Topshop do you:*

a) Keep it, no one will ever know

b) Hand it in to the police and hope no one else claims it so you can keep it or

c) Give it back to your enemy.

And I knew that my last thought was c) and it was the right answer and that I had to do it, I had to take it back. So after tea I put the envelope in a plastic bag and I said I needed to post something, it was another competition from a magazine. Mum said, 'As long as it's not for more hair dye, Billy. If I ever see hair dye again I think I will die – only with an I, not a Y.' And I said, 'It's not hair dye,' which wasn't even a lie.

And I meant to do it. I walked to the corner and past the clothes which were all gone now, but the concrete and car were still there, and through Kyle's gate which isn't an actual gate because that fell off two years ago it's just a gap, and I walked up the path and I was looking at the letterbox, just wondering if the envelope would fit, when the door opened and it was Kyle. He said, 'I thought I told you to piss off yesterday.' I said, 'I did.' And then a voice came from the house and it was Mrs Perry saying, 'Is that him?

Because you can tell him what I told him yesterday – to go back to hers and bloody stay there this time, we don't want him.' And I knew she didn't mean me. She meant Mr Perry. And I knew then that he was gone. And that if he was gone then I couldn't give the money back. So I said, 'Sorry, Kyle' and I went before he could say piss off again, or ask why I was standing there with a Discount Deals bag.

And when I got in I took the Discount Deals bag and what was in it back up to my room and I got into bed and I didn't need to count any glow stars or say Dogger or Fisher or Fastnet because I had done it. I had made my fortune. And now all I had to do was spend it.

Sunday
12th April

It's not as easy as you think spending £5,540. Not when it's Easter Sunday and you've got Nan and Mr Feinstein coming round for lunch and you're only allowed out for half an hour or the roast chicken will be dry. And Nan will complain because her chicken is never dry, even though she hasn't cooked a chicken for four years since Grandpa Stokes died, she only does boil in the bag or ready meals.

So I went to Mr Patel's and I bought eggs for everyone. Not chicken eggs because Mr Feinstein is allergic, i.e. if he has an egg he goes red and his throat closes and he can't breathe and someone has to inject him, but chocolate ones. I got Dairy Milk for Dave and Nan and Mr Feinstein and a Bounty one for Mum because it's the baby's favourite and Hannah Montana for Stan because it came in a mug with Miley Cyrus on it and Miley Cyrus is Stan's second favourite after Lady Gaga. I got four Creme Eggs for Big Lauren too for when she gets back, because she will have withdrawal symptoms like when she went to Swansea to see her cousin who got hit on the head and she had withdrawal symptoms from the chips at Fishcoteque. It cost £23.75 altogether which means I still have more than £5,516 left.

Mum asked where I got the money and I could feel my face getting red and hot then, but Nan said I'd probably saved Christmas money plus she gave me some money for grooming Tammy a couple of weeks ago which is true. And anyway Dave said, 'It doesn't matter where he got it, the point is he got you an egg, Jeanie.' And then Stan got upset because he hadn't got anyone eggs. Nan said it didn't matter because he was being good, but he said she was always saying being good was its own reward, so what was the point in that anyway? Dave said why didn't I do the 'Pokerface' song to show Nan, and Stan could be Big Lauren, and I was so happy at being excellent for buying eggs I said yes, and Stan was so happy to be allowed to be Lady Gaga he said yes too. And it turned out Stan is quite good at being Lady Gaga because he can make his voice go really high and really low and he knows all the dance moves and everything. Dave said it was actually quite funny and we should definitely audition for *Britain's Got Talent* and he could drive us to Bristol if we wanted. But I said Big Lauren can't do it because of being in Florida, so Stan said he would be Big Lauren but Mum said he can't be Big Lauren because it's Arthur Malik's *Pirates of the Caribbean* birthday party next Saturday, and besides Dave shouldn't encourage us. But Dave said, 'It's just some fun, Jeanie. I've always fancied being on telly, me.' But I said, 'It's all right because I don't want to do it on my own, thanks anyway.'

Because now I don't need to win. Not that, nor

the £10,000 or the year's supply of baby wipes or the romantic holiday for two. Because now I can buy everything I want.

Because I'm rich.

Monday
13th April

There are hardly any shops open on a bank holiday so Dave took me to Petworld on the ring road and I got a plastic hamster house shaped like a castle and a bag of monkey nuts. I'll get better things tomorrow though.

Dave said, 'Blimey, your nan pays well. Maybe I should quit my job and start working for her instead. I bet she's not as miserable as the Sister of No Mercy, either,' who is his boss and is Ward Sister Hawkins and who has a moustache. But I said he wouldn't like it that much because he would have to brush Tammy's bottom and he is a dog person, not a cat person. Plus then he would find out that Nan only pays me a pound and he would start wondering where the money came from. That's when I started feeling sick. I asked Dave to open the windows and he said, 'Too many eggs then, Billy boy?' and I nodded.

But it wasn't the eggs. It was the money.

When I got back me and Stan played with Lady and showed her her new house and fed her stuff, e.g. the monkey nuts but also a Discount Deals custard cream. Then she tried to eat a Vashta Nerada Top Trump, but that was OK because a Dalek will always beat it. Stan said Lady could be on *Britain's Got Talent* because she really will eat anything maybe even Simon Cowell, but I said I didn't think hamsters would be allowed because how would the Queen see her on the big stage when she does her act on the *Royal Variety Show* for instance. He is right that she will eat anything though because when he went upstairs for a wee I gave her a twenty-pound note and she ate it all, which is quite a useful skill for hiding evidence. I didn't give her any more though, because I don't want to hide any evidence. I want to spend it. And then the sick feeling in my stomach turned to warm. Because I knew that when I got to secondary school I wouldn't get my head flushed down the toilet because I would have the right trainers, and that if anyone came round to tea our beans wouldn't be Discount Deals any more they would be real ones, and we wouldn't have to watch just *Tracy Beaker* we could watch *Mythbusters* because now I can afford to buy Sky TV again.

And best of all, I don't need to count glow stars any more.

Because I can count money instead. £5482.

And that is the warmest feeling of all.

Tuesday
14th April

I didn't mean to buy all the stuff. It just sort of happened. Because Mum didn't want to go out because the baby had been kicking all night so she wanted to lie on the sofa and watch *This Morning* and Stan wanted to lie in with her because he likes the bit when they do the makeovers and transform people from ordinary mums into celebrities just with new haircuts and some make-up. So I said I was going round the corner to the park and maybe to Mr Patel's to get another Bounty and maybe a Mars bar. Mum said, 'Fine. But don't go spending a fortune, Billy.' I said, 'I won't.' And it wasn't a lie, because I didn't spend a fortune. Only £268.91.

Because I didn't go to the park, or to Mr Patel's. I went into town. And I'm not really supposed to go on my own, not till secondary school, but I did my Green Cross Code and I didn't talk to any strangers. I just went straight to Pemberton Games to get some new Top Trumps because Lady has eaten three now but then I noticed a DS and I thought I have to get one of those. Kyle Perry and Stephen Warren both have them and they are always going on about how awesome they are. And I remembered that Stephen Warren had got Sonic Super Collection so I got that too. And then it was like my brain and hands had been taken over by aliens because I got an MP3 player and some headphones like Sean Hawkes. And I bought Monopoly, which is a game where you buy roads in London with pretend money and then other people land on them and have to pay you rent. I always want to get Mayfair and Stan always wants Liverpool Street Station. Only we don't have Monopoly any more because Stan lost the metal iron and dog that go round the board, so we gave it to the charity shop. And last I got a radio shaped like a penguin only that is for Stan. And then I was hungry from all the shopping so I went to McDonald's which we are never allowed normally because it's expensive according to Mum, and is killing the world because of all the cows which are farting and causing global warming according to Dave. But Mum wasn't there and nor was Dave but Jake Palmer-Thomas was in there with his dad. He was getting a cheeseburger Happy Meal with a chocolate milkshake so I got the same because I was happy only I didn't drink all the milkshake because it's so thick you can't actually suck it up the straw without making your ears pop which I did four times and I got a free Smurfette which I don't even like but Stan does. Then I was so full with all the food inside me I could hardly carry the bags so I got a bus home even though Park Road, which is where McDonald's is, is only 724 metres away from our front door. Me and Big Lauren measured it once for a school project.

Mrs Peason from Peason's Bakery and also from

Beasley Street got on at the stop after me and she was going to sit next to me only there was no room, because of the bags, so she sat behind me instead. She said, 'Win the Lottery, did you, Billy?' and I said, 'No because I am not allowed to play the Lottery until I am sixteen, it's the law.' And she said, 'Oh, right. Well, you learn a new thing every day.' And at the time I was thinking that probably isn't true, because what if you were ill for instance and you just lay in bed and didn't watch telly or use the computer or read a book. So you wouldn't learn anything new, not even if a thousand bees can lift a laptop. But now I think maybe she was right after all. Because when I got home I did learn something new and that thing was hamsters do not eat twenty-pound notes after all.

I was upstairs hiding the stuff. I had put the Top Trumps next to my bed because Mum will not ask where they came from because they are only £3.99. Also she isn't interested in *Doctor Who*. I put the DS and Sonic and headphones and Monopoly and MP3 player at the back of the cupboard, which she doesn't open because she says it's like an explosion in a toy factory and last time a Ninja Turtle fell on her and poked her in the eye with his plastic claw. I put the rest of the money back under the mattress, and I was just wondering where I was going to hide a penguin-shaped radio when Mum shouted. She said, 'Billy Grimshaw-Jones, get down here this instant.' And I thought maybe she had X-ray eyes and had seen through the wall when I was running upstairs with the bags, or that she could see through the ceiling right now with me trying to put the penguin inside one of my shoes. But when I got into the front room it wasn't X-ray eyes. It was Lady.

Mum said, 'What the flaming hell is this?' And I said, 'I don't know' because I didn't know because it just looked like chewed-up paper. And Stan said, 'It's Lady's bed' because he had run downstairs too because of the shouting. And Mum said, 'I know that but what is it MADE of?' And she said the word 'made' really loudly like it was in capital letters because it was so important. And I looked and I saw why it was in capitals because the bed wasn't made of just bits of kitchen roll and some old computer paper where Dave had tried to print out WarRaiders cheats but the ink had run out. It was made of *Doctor Who* Top Trumps.

And money.

Stan said, 'Oh. My. God,' because saying 'Oh. My. God,' is big in Year 2 at the moment. But I didn't say that. Because I am Year 6. And because Mum had told Stan to stop saying it. And because I knew I had to say something else fast before I went red and gave it away so I said, 'It's fake, Mum. It's from Monopoly.' So Mum said, 'What Monopoly?' And I said, 'I got it in town, the other day,' which is only half a lie. And Mum said, 'Jesus, Billy. How much was that? Twenty quid?' And I said no it was £15.99 which isn't a lie at all. But Mum didn't care about that. She cared about the money. She said this wasn't a time to be spending money on board games and if I wanted it that bad I could have borrowed it off Dave 2 or even Big Lauren. But I said Big Lauren has Coronation Street Monopoly and that's not the same, which it isn't because who wants to own Roy's Rolls for instance? And also it's good that Lady wasn't chewing up real money. But Mum didn't agree. She said, 'You're spending a fortune on junk, Billy, and I've barely got a tenner in my purse. This has to stop. Any money left over from Christmas or whatever you save up you use for something important. Do you understand me? Do you?' And I nodded and she said good, and she went upstairs to her room with the chewed-up twenty-pound note still in her hand and shut the door.

And Stan said 'Ace' because then he got to watch *Tracy Beaker* instead of *Escape to the Country*. But I didn't feel like it. Not today. Because I had to do something. I had to count the money.

I counted it four times and each time it was the same amount, i.e. £5,213 because I had put all the small coins in the charity dog outside Mr Patel's. And then I thought that Mum was right about something which is that it's mad I am spending money on toys when there is important stuff to buy. Only I'm not sure what that is yet. So then I thought well she can decide, i.e. I can put the money into her purse. Not all of it. Because it won't fit. And also because she will be suspicious. But if I just put a small amount in at a time then she will just think it's her going mad from the baby, e.g. last week she forgot it was even Wednesday, so she will think she just forgot she had it in the first place.

So I did it. I put twenty pounds in in two ten pound notes. Because that's enough to go shopping at Sainsbury's. And enough to buy some Bounties. And enough to make the coldness inside me turn into warm.

And that's when I knew Nan was wrong when she said money couldn't make you happy. Because I knew it could. It could make me happy and it could make Mum happy. And I was going to make sure it did.

Wednesday 15th April

The money didn't make Mum happy. It made her and Dave have a row.

What happened was that we had just picked up Stan from Arthur Malik's and we were driving down Mason Road when Mum said, 'That's odd.' And I said 'What's odd?' and she said, 'The red light's on,' which is the warning light. I said she had better go to Broadley Mechanics which is the garage on the ring road and Mum said, 'This is all I need, a hundred pounds on the flaming car.' And I said it might not be a hundred pounds it might only be forty for instance but Mum said nothing was ever only forty pounds when it came to cars. And she was right. Because we did go to Broadley Mechanics and a man whose name was Chas, which I know because it was sewn on his overall in a patch, said it was the filter and it would be at least a hundred pounds and no we couldn't just drive the car because what if it blew up with kids in it. So Mum said, 'Fine,' only then we were stuck on the ring road which is 4.5 miles from home. So I said we could get a taxi and she said we couldn't, because we didn't have enough money, and I said we might. She said, 'For God's sake, Billy, that's enough. I'll just call Dave, he's due off in a minute anyway.' And so she did and Dave came to get us and he was cross because the Sister of No Mercy was cross. He said, 'Couldn't you have just called a cab?' And Mum said no because she didn't have any cash and I said she did. And she said, 'No I flaming don't.' And she got out her purse to prove it only she couldn't prove it because there was two ten-pound notes.

And so she said, 'What the hell is this?' And Dave

said, 'It's twenty quid. Jesus. I've just pissed off the Sister of No Mercy because I was supposed to be doing overtime and you had twenty quid all along.' And Mum said, 'But it's not mine.' And Dave said, 'Well, whose is it, then? The Queen of Flaming Sheba's?' And Mum said, 'Did you put this in here?' And Dave said, 'Yes, because I'm just made of money. I just go round hiding it in your purse. There's probably fifty in your make-up bag and another hundred in your knicker drawer. Christ.' And then no one said anything else until we got home, which is when Dave said, 'We might as well sell the car anyway. No point keeping it now you're not working.' And Mum didn't say, 'No because how am I going to take Billy to the swimming pool or Stan to Arthur Malik's and anyway what about when I get a new job, e.g. at the new multiplex which is 7.8 miles away according to Google.' She just said, 'Fine,' and went up to the bedroom and Dave went back out again, but not in the car this time just on his feet.

He didn't come back for five hours and forty-one

minutes which I know because I was lying in bed and looking at the time on my glow-in-the-dark watch. And I heard Mum say, 'Where have you been?' And Dave said, 'Don't start, Jeanie.' And then I heard Mum come back up the stairs. I know it was her not Dave because she takes twenty-five seconds on average because of the baby and Dave takes ten and I timed it. And also because the TV went on downstairs and it was *Top Gear* and Mum doesn't like *Top Gear* because she says the men are all show-offs.

And then I thought what if my money doesn't buy happiness after all? What if my money is cursed like the tomb of Tutankhamun and all it can buy is BAD?

And I counted it again. I counted it five times. And each time there was £5,193 which is still a fortune.

But I didn't feel warm this time. I felt cold and scared. Because £5,193 could buy a whole lot of BAD.

Thursday 16th April

Three more BAD things happened today.

Stan moved into my room.

Mum found the penguin radio.

There has been a robbery.

It started at breakfast. Dave and Mum were having another row, only not about the money this time but about why Dave hadn't done any of the things on his list of things to do which is stuck on the fridge with a magnet shaped like a melon. He was supposed to *Clear out the garage* and *Sell exercise bike* (because no one exercises on it except Stan when he is pretending to be ET on the bicycle) and *Paint nursery*, i.e. Stan's room. Dave said give him a chance because he'd only just got up and yesterday he'd been at work and then ferrying us back from the mechanics and the day before that he'd had to cover Dave 2's shift because he had been at an Ultimate Frisbee match in Cardiff. Mum said, 'There's always an excuse.' And Dave said, 'They're not excuses, they're reasons. It's not the same.' And I checked on Google and he is right, but Mum didn't think so, which is why Dave moved the bed into my room before he went to work. This is why Mum found the penguin because it was under my bed but not under the mattress, and she was checking for pants. She said, 'Where the hell did you get this?' And I said, 'I swapped it.' And Mum said, 'What for?' And I said my piece of quartz from Wookey Hole, which isn't true because Big Lauren has it because she says crystals have healing powers and so all celebrities have crystals, but Mum believed it anyway because Stan swapped his Optimus Prime for a packet of Rolos with Arthur Malik yesterday and she said we were a pair of eejits with no concept of the value of money. But I didn't say, 'Actually I'm not and there is a DS and a game and an MP3 player and Monopoly at the back of the cupboard and £5193 under my mattress.' I said, 'Can I go round Nan's? It's bingo,' and Mum said yes and to take Stan because she was sick of us getting under her feet, so I did.

And Nan didn't win at bingo this week so we didn't go to Slice O'Heaven we went to Mr Patel's to buy some fishfingers and also a Broadley Echo for Nan. This is so she can check to see who is dead and who is in court because she likes to keep an eye out for criminals which is where we saw about the robbery.

It was at Bright Sparks which is the welder's on the ring road. Someone had taken the safe. Not even opened it just taken the whole thing with all the money inside. Nan said, 'Nearly six thousands pounds gone. It's the recession, that's why all the crime is happening, I blame the prime minister.' Only she blames the prime minister for everything, even the time she spilt a tin of rice pudding on the floor, because she said if she had a better pension she would be buying chocolate mousse not Ambrosia. Only it wasn't the prime minister then and it wasn't him now, because how would he know where to find the safe in a welder's in Broadley?

And that's when the thought began. A tiny black thought that began with, 'But Kyle's dad would know, because he works there'.

But I didn't want the thought to carry on and get bigger so I tried to concentrate on something else, i.e. the fish I am eating is cod which can grow up to 1.8 metres long and live until it's thirty. Once in Australia they cut open a cod and inside was a whole human head. But even though I was thinking this I could still hear the other thought beneath it, whispering, and I could also hear Brenda Gilhooly who was in the front room with Nan say, 'I knew it because I saw a beetle in my tea leaves and I thought it was about Jac Naylor on *Holby* on Tuesday but it must have been about the robbery on Thursday instead. I should hire myself out to the police.' And Nan said, 'You should, Bren,' and laughed. But I didn't. I started to choke on the piece of cod and Nan had to slap me on the back and it flew out of my mouth and it hit the cat calendar which is pictures of cats in costumes and it was a tabby in a pink waistcoat and Nan said, 'That's better. You can breathe now.'

But she was wrong. I couldn't breathe. Because the little thought had got bigger. So big it was bursting out of my chest so that no air could fit in. And the thought was this: 'The robbery was the night before Good Friday. The night before Kyle's mum and dad had the big row and she threw all his stuff out of the house. The night before I found the money.'

I couldn't sleep because of the bad feeling. And I couldn't count the money to make the bad feeling go away because Stan was in the bed next to me and he wakes up at anything even if a pigeon does a loud coo outside the window for instance.

I didn't want to count it anyway. I wanted to forget it. To forget I had it all. But it wouldn't let me. It kept talking to me. Whispering things in a bad man's voice like Darth Vadar. It said, 'Mr Perry stole us. And we were cursed so now he and Mrs Perry have broken up.' And it said, 'And now we will curse you, and your mum and Dave will break up.' And worst of all it said, 'And you will go to prison because you have the evidence. Not Mr Perry. You, Billy Grimshaw-Jones.'

And I told it to stop. I said, 'Shut up, shut up, shut up,' in my head over and over. But it didn't shut up. It said, 'You will be inside a cell and it won't even be like a care home. It won't be like *Tracy Beaker*. It won't be painted yellow and purple and there won't be bunk beds, it will be grey and cold and there will be gruel for breakfast and lunch and dinner and if you say, "Please sir can I have some more" you will be sent to sleep in a coffin.' And every word got louder and louder until I thought Stan would hear it and say, 'Why is there a voice like Darth Vadar coming from the mattress?'

And even though he didn't, even though his eyes were tight shut and his mouth was wide open and his monkey with the one eye called Dora was in his left hand I knew someone else would be able to hear it.

Or see it. Not in real life maybe. But in their tea.

Brenda Gilhooly would look at the bottom of the Charles and Diana mug and there it would be, in broken up PG Tips. And she would say, 'I know who it was. I know who has the money – it's Billy Grimshaw-Jones. It's all here in the tea leaves.'

And then I didn't care if we were so poor we only ever shopped at Discount Deals. I didn't care if we had to sell both cars and walk everywhere even to the ring road. I didn't care if I had to wear daps to school and got my head flushed down the toilet every day. I just knew I had to get rid of the money.

Before it got rid of me.

Friday
17th April

It's hard finding over £5,000. But it's even harder trying to lose it. I wished then that hamsters did eat money because then I could have just fed it all to Lady and she would have eaten the evidence, but she wasn't eating anything not even hamster food. Stan said she was sad because she was missing Big Lauren, but Mum said it was because Stan had fed her chocolate porridge and hamsters are not designed to eat chocolate porridge.

And I was sad for Lady but not that sad because it meant that Mum was busy trying to cheer Stan up by making him boiled egg and soldiers and I could get out of the house without anyone saying, 'Where are you going with your Tardis rucksack, Billy? There's no school today.' And so I wouldn't have to say, 'I'm going to post £5193 through Kyle Perry's letterbox because his dad stole it from the welder's and then I stole it from him.'

But I couldn't in the end. Post the money I mean. Because when I got to Kyle's he was sitting on the wall kicking it with the back of his Nike boot so it was all scuffed which is mad because they cost £89.98 so that is £44.99 ruined but I didn't say that I said, 'All right, Kyle.' And he said, 'No.'

And I knew why. Because his dad was gone. Because of the money. And I knew that if I gave it back to them then only more bad would come of it because Nan was right and being rich is nothing but bad luck. And besides there would be £367 missing so I would get arrested anyway so I needed another plan.

And I thought all day. I thought I could open a bank account in someone else's name, e.g. David

Smith and put it in there and just leave it until the people at the bank start thinking this is odd why doesn't David Smith ever come to collect his money and they tell the police and the police will realise it's the stolen money and try to arrest David Smith only he doesn't exist. But I checked on Google and I can't open an account without my mum and at least two pieces of identification. And I don't have any identification that says David Smith, I only have my passport from the time we went to Spain when I was seven, and that says Billy Grimshaw. Anyway, Mum doesn't want to go out because she's not feeling right.

Then I thought maybe I could give all the money to a charity, e.g. the dog's home and they could use it to say buy some new leads or a kennel. But then I remembered that the slot in the dog collection box outside Mr Patel's is only big enough for coins and the one inside the actual dog's home where you can put notes is right in front of the desk. Plus Mr Hirst is sometimes at the desk and he lives next door to Donna Rhymes who is Big Lauren's mum's best friend and Donna would be bound to tell her. Then she would tell Big Lauren and it would be all over school, which would mean Jake Palmer-Thomas would know and his dad is a policeman.

Then I thought maybe I could bury the money because it's not coins it's paper, so no one not even Alan would find it with his metal detector. So I thought of all the places I could bury it like in Nan's garden. Or in the park. Or on the piece of mud at the back of Gaskell's. But then I thought that even if I buried it in say Bristol Brenda Gilhooly would still find it, i.e. she would see it in her tea leaves.

And I would still hear it talking to me. Whispering the curse. Saying my name.

And I knew then I had to take it far away. So far no one would find it, or me. And then I thought about *Titanic*. But not about Jack this time, who goes to America to find his fortune. But about Rose who goes to lose hers. Because when she gets there she could say she was Rose DeWitt Bukater and engaged to Caledon Hockley and she would be rich for ever. But she doesn't. She lies and says she is Rose

Dawson. And even though it means she will be poor, she doesn't care. Because she is free.

And then I thought about Big Lauren in Florida in the house with five bedrooms and a swimming pool and a parakeet. And I thought that Garth and Sharon and Todd and Chip don't actually need five bedrooms all the time so I could live in one of them for a bit. And I knew exactly how to get there because Big Lauren had given me the address for Lady to write to her.

And I knew then that I had to go to America. Only not by boat like Rose, because that would take seven days. But by aeroplane, like Big Lauren.

Because it's only seven hours from Bristol Airport.

Which is right next to Cabot Hotel.

Which is where the *Britain's Got Talent* audition is tomorrow.

Saturday 18th April

I told Dave I had changed my mind. He was still in bed because it was Saturday and me and Stan are supposed to watch cartoons until at least nine o'clock so Mum and Dave can have a lie-in. Big Lauren says it's so they can have 'me' time but I said Mum would be mental to want 'me' time with Dave first thing in the morning because his breath smells and also *Rastamouse* is on. She wasn't having 'me' time this morning anyway she was still asleep and Dave was reading a magazine about nurses even though he is one so he should know all about them.

I said, 'You know you said you would drive me to the audition if I changed my mind? Well I have. You don't have to stay because Casey Webster is there and he is swallowing a live goldfish only not really. His mum will be able to vouch for me because you have to have an adult to vouch for you at all times. Only you have to get up right now because it starts at ten o'clock and there might be queues.'

I had thought of everything, you see.

I had thought I needed to pack my Longleat T-shirt in case the weather is hotter in America, and *Oliver Twist* so I can do some homework, and my glow stars even though I don't think they'll let me stick them on the ceiling in the plane but not my shampoo because that isn't allowed in case I am a terrorist who is going to throw it at the pilot for instance.

I had thought I don't need to cry when I say goodbye because once I have lost the fortune I can come back again and I will be the prodigal son like in the Bible. Everyone will be so pleased I am back they will not wonder if it was me who had the robbery money at all. But I am glad Mum was still asleep because if she had said, 'Good luck, Billy and remember it's not about winning and you'll always be my champion,' which is what she did before sports day and the swimming gala and football the time we lost seven-nil to St Julian's, then some tears would have definitely come out. Stan didn't say goodbye at all though because he was too busy being cross that he wasn't allowed to the audition because of the pirate party. He wanted it to be a pop-star party so he could go as Lady Gaga so Dave said maybe he could go as Lady Gaga in a pirate outfit because it's the sort of mad thing she might wear and he cheered up a bit then.

And I had thought I had better be quiet all the way in the car to the hotel in case I blurt something out but it is fine because Dave will think it is just because I am nervous about the audition and he did he just sang to a song on the radio about wearing the same jeans for four days in a row which Mum would never let him do in real life because he is always getting stuff on them.

And I had thought I needed to say, 'I just need to go to the loo, I always need to go to the loo when I am nervous' to Casey Webster's mum, just when Casey is about to go in so that they can't come with me. That's when I can make a run for it to the door and then there is a free shuttle bus to the airport every fifteen minutes. And it worked because Mrs Webster said, 'Well OK, Billy, but don't be long or you'll miss your place in the queue and then it will be the back of the line for you, and then God knows how long you'll be here – there are at least twenty tap-dancers, and a man who can lick his own nose. And I've got to get back to take a casserole round to Mrs Higginson by two.' And I said, 'It's fine because look I can see Karen Connolly's mum and why don't I wait with her now instead? You have been very kind and I hope Casey gets through.' And she said, 'Fat chance. I thought you were bursting for a wee, Billy, hadn't you better go because you don't want to go in with wet trousers it'll show up something rotten on that polyester.'

And so I did go. But not to the loo to the bus. The driver said, 'You going to be a star then? Like that Justin Bieber?' I said, 'No, I didn't get through. But it doesn't matter. Money isn't everything you know and it can't buy you happiness.' And he said, 'No, but it'll buy you a big enough car to drive right up to it.' Which I didn't understand but it didn't matter because we were there at the airport.

But what I hadn't thought of was who would be at the airport when I got there.

What I hadn't thought of was Stacey.

I forgot she had a new job. Because when I got to the front of the queue for Flyby there she was in her too-red lipstick and too-orange face saying, 'Billy Grimshaw-Jones what the flamin' heck are you doing here? Does your mum know you're in Bristol? How is she anyway? Jesus, three kids, she must be mental. That dog is enough for me and he pooed on the carpet again last night, can you believe it?' And I could because he is always doing it but I didn't say so I said, 'Yes she does and I am going to America to stay with Big Lauren's aunt Sharon and uncle Garth. They have five bedrooms and a swimming pool and it's all planned, so can I have a ticket to Miami please?' And Stacey said, 'Are you serious?' And I said,

'Yes.' And she said, 'Well, you can't fly direct, you have to go via New York, and that flight's not until two o'clock and it's all booked up. I mean, there might be a cancellation so you could always wait. Why don't you do that, eh, Billy? Why don't you leave your passport with me right here where it's safe, you go and have a nice cup of tea, and come back in an hour and I'll see what I can do.'

And the thing is I believed her. Because when she said she could get me a *Doctor Who* water bottle for school off her friend Horse-Face John that was true. And when she said she used to be West of England rhythm gymnastics champion before she discovered boys and doughnuts that was true. And so I believed she was going to do what she said and find me a cancelled ticket and so I did go and I had a Coca-Cola because I didn't fancy a cup of tea not even a nice one.

And that's when I heard it again. I heard the money. It said, 'Running away won't help, Billy. It won't change anything. Because the police will still look for you.' But I thought as hard as I could back at it. I thought, 'As soon as I am on the plane I am free because the air belongs to nobody so nobody will be able to arrest me.' So the money said, 'But you'll miss home, Billy. You'll be all alone with no one.'

And even though I tried to think back, 'No I won't,' it didn't work. Because the money was right. I would miss Mum and her tummy stuck out with the baby-hand under the skin and wanting Bounty bars even at breakfast. And I would miss Dave saying, 'Button time, Billy,' every time Hutch Hathaway says, 'It's madness'. And I would miss Stan even though he has dropped Bionicles all over my room and even though he likes women's magazines and wants to be Lady Gaga. And I would miss the house even, like Mum said that time. I would miss the airing cupboard where we grew orange pips and where I used to hide in Hide and Seek with my dad. I would miss the hot tap in the bathroom that comes on too hard and always splashes you and it's always a shock no matter how many times it happens. And most of all I would miss the kitchen with the magnet on the fridge shaped like a melon and the treat cupboard and everyone sat at the table arguing about whether or not you could make a glider out of concrete.

And I could feel a dark cold seed inside me start to grow like an orange pip only it wasn't taking three weeks it was taking three seconds. Its leaves crushed against my chest so that each breath was hard, and stalks snaked inside my head so the tears started to fall out and roll down my cheeks, because there was no room inside any more. And I thought. I thought hard for something warm that would shrink the dark seed plant and dry the tears and I thought that Mum had said something else and that was that, 'Life is like that sometimes. You don't get happy endings, you just have to make the best of it.' And I thought that is what I was doing, i.e. making the best of it. That was all I had tried to do all the time with the competitions and even with Mr Perry's money. I was just trying to make the best of it all. And the only way to do that now was to go to America so that Stan could stay at home and Mum and Dave wouldn't break up and I wouldn't be arrested.

But Stacey didn't know that. Stacey thought I was being the worst I could be.

That's why she lied.

I didn't see him at first, I felt him. Standing behind the red plastic seats. But I knew it was him because he smelt of Pears soap and coffee and when he slipped into the chair next to mine 'he said, 'So you've done it again, then, Billy.' And he didn't shout or hit me like Mr Perry would have done. He sucked up the last bit of the Coca-Cola and until it made a slurping noise which Mum never ever lets us do because it's rude. And I wanted to smile but I couldn't because smiles need warm and all I had was cold and darkness and the money whispering in the Darth Vadar voice saying, 'Run, Billy, run. You have to get out of here, now. It doesn't matter where, just do it. Just run.' But I knew I couldn't. Because my legs were shaking and my hands too. And I knew what would stop them and the cold. I knew he was strong and warm because he had a heart that was as twice as big as normal men according to Mum, and

146

I knew he was Luke Skywalker and he would win but he was waiting, just waiting like Luke Skywalker, waiting for me to say one word, and I did, I said it.

I said, 'Dave.'

And when the word came out, it was like a champagne cork that had popped because then all the crying and the shaking burst out of me too and I thought it would never stop. I thought I would be there on the red plastic seat at Burger King for ever not being able to walk or talk or even drink Coca-Cola. But the more I shook the tighter Dave held me, and the more he said, 'It's going to be OK, Billy, you'll see. It's all going to be OK.' Until he had said the words so many times that he had whispered all the darkness and cold out and all that was left was me shivering with some snot coming out of my nose and he wiped it with a Whopper napkin and smiled and said, 'Righto then, kid. Do you want to tell me what's going on?'

And it wasn't a rhetorical question. He actually wanted an answer. And the thing is I wanted to give him one. Because every time I told him a fact, like about being poor and wearing daps for football and buying stuff at Discount Deals, I felt the seed shrivel and warm coming back into my body. Into my fingers and toes at first but then creeping up my arms and legs. And so I told him more. I told him about Mrs Perry and the clothes, and the envelope, and the DS and the Monopoly. And I told him how I meant to take the money back but there was the robbery and then Mr Perry disappeared. And I told him about the care home and how I didn't want to be in there in case it wasn't like *Tracy Beaker* after all, and then I felt the warm touch the edges of my chest. So I told him about how the money talked to me and how it was saying things and that the only way to make it quiet was to go to America like Rose so I can be free.

And that's when Dave said, 'Oh Billy Grimshaw-Jones. You really are a one.' And he smiled and kissed me on the top of my head. And I didn't care that at secondary school you don't let anyone kiss you. Not even your mum. And definitely not a vegetarian nurse who likes comics and isn't even your real dad.

Because the warm had spread to my stomach. And that was all down to Dave.

Then he said something else. Another whisper. It was, 'Is the money still talking now?' And I listened, I listened really hard to all the noises in the air. I could hear a *bing bong* and then a woman saying, 'Passengers for Flight C eight-seven-nine please go to Boarding Gate D.' And I could hear a boy saying, 'How long now? Is it nearly time? Is it?' And I could hear a woman saying, 'Do you want fries with that?' And a man say, 'I would have asked if I did, wouldn't I?' back to her.

But I couldn't hear the money. I couldn't hear the Darth Vadar voice. Not a single word. And so I shook my head. And Dave said, 'Is it in there?' And he nodded at the rucksack and I said, 'Yes.' And he said, 'How much is left?' And I said, '£5193'. And Dave said, 'Crikey. OK, well we can deal with that later, but first of all let's get you home, Billy boy.' I said, 'Does Mum know?' And Dave said, 'No. Which is a flaming miracle. Stacey may look like a walking satsuma but she had the sense to call me instead. Good job and all because your mum's not feeling too bright today, so maybe we'll keep this between me and you for now, eh?' And I said yes because I didn't want anyone but Dave to know the whole truth. Not Stacey. Not Stan. Not Big Lauren. And definitely not Mum. I just wanted to get home and smell her smell of blue roll-on deodorant and coconut shampoo and listen to her moan about having to wee and see her get me a digestive down from the cupboard even a Discount Deals one and touch her tummy with the baby breathing inside.

But in the end none of that happened because when we got back Mum was gone.

There was a note on the fridge under the magnet shaped like a melon. It said, *Baby coming. Gone to hospital. Why aren't you answering your bloody phone?* And Dave said a really bad swear but I didn't even say a word because the baby was coming only it wasn't due not for six weeks and that meant something was wrong.

★ ★ ★

I don't even remember driving to the hospital now. Or what was on the telly in the waiting room. Or even what the nurse said to me when she came and sat down on the plastic chair next to me.

All I can remember is them in that room. Mum all sweaty in a blue gown with mascara on her cheeks and Dave with tears on his and both of them pale and grey. And I was waiting for the words like on *Holby City* again. The ones that make worlds fall apart. I was waiting for, 'I'm sorry, Billy.'

But it wasn't words I heard. It was a sound. High and squawly. Like a kitten or a bird.

Or a baby.

It was tiny, as tiny as a kitten, and it didn't look like a normal baby in a stretchy suit with fat cheeks and a hat, it was just in a nappy and in a glass tank like a fish and there was a tube going in its nose and more in its arms and chest.

But it was alive. Completely alive. Because every little while it would make the kitten noise and wave its arm, and that's when I saw it. The see-through plastic bracelet the size of a ring. And inside it were words and those words said, *Baby Girl Jones.*

And in that moment I knew the world would never fall apart. Not for any of us. That she would hold it together. Even if we were on the breadline and I got beaten up at secondary school for wearing daps and had to count the glow stars eleven times. She would make it all right. Because she was worth more than money. She was the fortune. Our fortune.

Our Rose Jones.

And the warm flooded my heart like soup.

Sunday
27th September

The name was my idea.

Big Lauren said actually it was hers because she had put it on the list in January only she had said Rose DeWitt DiCaprio Jones which isn't the same at all. Stan says she should be called Lady after Lauren's hamster because it was dead now because of eating its own house so it didn't matter but Mum said it was still a weird name for a baby and anyway wasn't the new hamster being called Lady but Lauren said, 'No, it's Dexter. He's in my class at secondary school and I'm going to marry him but not in Paris because we're doing Spanish instead and so he won't know how to say "I do".'

Secondary school isn't so bad after all. Only we don't even call it secondary school now, we just call it Broadley Comp, otherwise we would get our heads flushed down the toilet. Even though I don't know anyone who has actually had that done. Stephen Warren says a boy in his class called Luke Seward says his cousin's best friend's brother got it done last Thursday. But he also says he is related to Simon Cowell, so it's probably a lie.

Kyle Perry hasn't got his head flushed. Not at our school anyway. He's gone away for a bit with his mum. Nan said they're in prison for being accomplices to the robbery, but they're not, they're in Clevedon with his aunt. It wasn't Mr Perry who broke into the welder's anyway it was a man called James Kelsey from Yate, who was already wanted for similar incidents at Charlie's Autospares and Poundworld according to the *Broadley Echo*.

Nan says I shouldn't believe what I read because they've got it wrong before like when they said vandals had sawn through the wires in the Salvation Army shop and it turned out it was squirrels, but Brenda knew because she saw a squirrel in her tea.

She says Brenda sees everything, e.g. she can see that Rose is going to be a beauty when she grows up – a real beauty.

But she didn't see that I would get put in the top stream for English even though my essay wasn't even true.

And she didn't see that Stan would decide he is definitely not into Lady Gaga or Hannah Montana or even *Man Versus Food* any more, he is into *Deadliest Catch* like Jake Palmer-Thomas. Jake is now first toughest in the infants because Seth Makepeace has gone to special school.

And she didn't see *Money Madness*.

The letter came through four days after we got back from the hospital. Dave wasn't going to do it because he said he didn't care about money all he cared about was Mum and me and Stan and Rose. But Mum said go on because he'd always wanted to be on telly so he did. And he won £10,000. It would have been more but they asked him what TARDIS stands for and he didn't know so he rang his phone-a-friend which was Dave 2 and he said he didn't know it stood for anything when actually it is Time And Relative Dimension In Space and even I knew that which I said to Dave when he got home but he said, 'It doesn't matter, Billy, we've got a fortune anyway.'

And we have. Or at least enough to repair the Toyota Corolla so that Mum can still take Stan to Arthur Malik's and do the big shop at Discount Deals, because they do the best chocolate and even Nan agrees.

And enough to pay back the rest of the money I owed to Mr Perry. Mum said he'll only bet it on the horses again but Dave said that's not the point and he can spend it on a lifetime's supply of candy floss if he wants it won't make him any happier.

And I know he's right and that stuff doesn't change anything. Not really. I know Nike is just a label and that there is loads of good stuff on telly not just on Sky TV. And I know custard creams still taste sweet even if the packet says *Fondant Sandwich Biscuits* on it.

But people are wrong when they say money doesn't change anything either. Because Dave asked what we should do with the rest of it. He said if we wanted we could build a small room on top of the kitchen called an extension and it would be a bedroom for Stan so we wouldn't have to share.

Or, he had another idea.

And the other idea turned out to be brilliant. Because now we have bunk beds which are just like on *Tracy Beaker* only better because they're not in the Dumping Ground, they're in our own house at 23 Brunel Street. And Justine isn't in the next-door bedroom, it's Mum and Dave, and next door to that is Rose.

And Granny Grimshaw has someone to come in and help her so she doesn't forget stuff, e.g. to get washed or eat her tea.

And best of all, the special care unit at the hospital has a new bed for babies who are born too early like Rose, which amazingly is the same price as an extension.

But it buys a lot more happiness.

Joanna Nadin is a former journalist and government speechwriter. She has written several award-winning books for younger readers, as well as the best-selling Rachel Riley series for teens. She lives in Bath with her daughter. Visit www.joannanadin.com to find out more.

★

**Find out how Billy became
Billy Grimshaw-Jones in:**

★

Discover more books you'll love at
www.piccadillypress.co.uk